Also by

CARLO LUCARELLI

Carte Blanche

THE DAMNED
SEASON

Carlo Lucarelli

THE DAMNED
SEASON

*Translated from the Italian
by Michael Reynolds*

Europa
editions

Europa Editions
116 East 16th Street
New York, N.Y. 10003
www.europaeditions.com
info@europaeditions.com

Copyright © 1991 by Sellerio Editore, Palermo
First Publication 2007 by Europa Editions

Translation by Michael Reynolds
Original Title: *L'estate torbida*
Translation copyright © 2007 by Europa Editions

Library of Congress Cataloging in Publication Data is available
ISBN 978-1-933372-27-3

Lucarelli, Carlo
The Damned Season

Book design by Emanuele Ragnisco
www.mekkanografici.com

Printed in Italy
Arti Grafiche La Moderna – Rome

CONTENTS

PREFACE - 13

THE DAMNED SEASON - 17

ABOUT THE AUTHOR - 119

Translator's Note

Two acronyms appearing in what follows have not been translated so as to maintain the natural flow of the narrative. CLN, first appearing on page 19, stands for the *Comitato di Liberazione Nazionale* (National Liberation Committee). Founded in 1943, the CLN was a conglomerate of anti-fascist political parties and organizations that coordinated the Resistance during wartime Italy. The CLN was dissolved in 1947. GAP, first appearing on page 55, stands for *Gruppi di azione patriottica* (Patriotic Action Groups), regional Resistance cells operating in wartime Italy.

Some forget that less than a year has passed since we were risking our lives every day, since our comrades left their homes to shoot, since they were tortured in Villa Trieste . . . At that time, when Communists were shooting and dying for everyone, nobody told them they mustn't "overdo it" . . .

L'Unità,* 2 November 1945

Let us lay down our arms, for we took up arms to chase the Germans out and the Germans are now gone . . . We do not long for adventure, we have no desire for parades, we went to war and we won, now our job is not to lose the peace.

L'Unità, 31 May 1945

---

* Italian Communist Party's national daily newspaper. (Tr.)

I was supposed to graduate from Bologna University with a thesis in contemporary history on the police during the fascist period. I don't remember well what studies had brought me there, but I was collecting material for a thesis entitled "The Vision of the Police in the Memories of Anti-Fascists" when I ran across a strange character who in a certain sense changed my life.

He was a policeman who had spent forty years in the Italian police, from 1941 to 1981, when he retired. He had started in the fascist political police, the OVRA, a secret organization the meaning of whose very acronym was never known with certainty. As an "ovrino," he told me, his job was to tail, to spy on, and to arrest anti-fascists who were plotting against the regime. Later, still as an ovrino, he was to tail, to spy on, and to arrest those fascists who disagreed with fascism's leader, Benito Mussolini. During the war, his job went back to tailing, spying on, and arresting anti-fascist saboteurs, but towards the end of the war, when part of liberated Italy was under the control of partisan formations fighting alongside the Allies, my strange policeman friend actually became part of the partisan police. As he was good, he told me, he had never done anything particularly brutal and the partisans needed professionals like him to ensure public order and safety. Naturally, his duties included arresting fascists who had stained themselves with criminal acts during the war. Several years later, when, following elections, a regular government was formed in Italy, our policeman became part of the Italian Republic's police; his job, to tail, to spy on, and to arrest some of those partisans who had been his colleagues and who were now considered dangerous subversives.

That encounter, and the studies I was undertaking at that moment, opened my eyes to a period that is fundamental in the history of Italy: strange, complicated and contradictory, as were the final years of the fascist regime in Italy.

Benito Mussolini and the fascists took power in October, 1922. For twenty years, the regime consolidated itself into a ferocious dictatorship that suspended political and civil liberties, dissolved parties and newspapers, persecuted opponents and put practically all of Italy in uniform, like what was happening in the meantime in Hitler's Germany. The outbreak of World War II saw Italy allied with Nazi Germany, but a series of military defeats, the hostility of a people exhausted by the war effort, and the landing of the Anglo-American forces in Sicily in 1943, brought about the fall of the fascist regime. Mussolini was arrested and, on September 8, the new government decided to break the alliance with Hitler and carry on the war alongside the Allies.

At this point, Italy splits in two as the German Army occupies that part of the country not yet liberated by the advance of the Anglo-American forces and puts Benito Mussolini in charge of a collaborationist government. This is one of the hardest and most ferocious moments in Italy's history. There is the war stalled on the North Italian front, where there is fierce fighting, for at least a year. There is dread of the *Brigate Nere*, the Black Brigades, and the formations of the new fascist government's political police who, together with the German SS, repress sabotage activities and resistance by partisan formations. There is, above all, enormous moral and political confusion that combines the desperation of those who know they are losing, the opportunism of those ready to change sides, the guilelessness of those who haven't understood anything, and even the desire for revenge in those who are about to arrive.

Only a couple of years, until April, 1945, when the war in Italy ends, but two ferocious, bloody, and above all confusing years, as I learned thanks to my studies and the accounts of my policeman friend. In Milan alone, for example, there were at least sixteen different police forces, from the regular police, the "Questura," to the Gestapo, each doing as they pleased and sometimes arresting one another.

But above all, I understood one thing from that encounter. For, after having heard that man recount forty years of his life in the Italian political police, during which with every change of government he found himself having to tail, to spy on, and to arrest those who had previously been his bosses, the question came spontaneously to me: "Excuse me, Maresciallo, but . . . who do you vote for?" And he, with equal spontaneity, responded: "What does that have to do with it? I'm a policeman." As if to say: I don't take political stands. I do. I am a technician, a professional, not a politician.

At that point, I thought that there are moments in the life of a country in which the technicians and the professionals are also asked to account for their political choices and nonchoices. I thought about what my policeman friend would have done if things had gone differently. And to ask oneself what would have happened if is the spring that triggers the idea for a novel.

So I started writing *Carte Blanche*. I invented Commissario De Luca, protagonist of *Carte Blanche*, *The Damned Season* and *Via delle Oche*, and lost myself in his adventures.

And I never did write my thesis.

Carlo Lucarelli

CHAPTER ONE

There was a land mine in the middle of the trail. Somebody had dug around the edges, exposing its curved, shiny contours, and had planted a stick next to it with a red rag tied to the top. Whoever it was had also dug underneath a little, and there, in that precise spot, ants had made a hole—perfectly round with a bulging rim and that gray metal covering for a roof. Sitting on a rock, his trench coat folded over his knees, De Luca watched them madly going in and out of the ant hole. One was trying to climb up onto his shoe and somehow it looked like it was returning his gaze, tilting its head back on its inexistent neck, antennas gyrating frenetically.

"They sense the storm coming," said a voice behind him. De Luca jumped to his feet with a frightened gasp. A man was standing there, tall, young, with curly hair, wearing a leather flyer's jacket. De Luca noticed that he was armed—an old canvas military holster was sticking out from under his jacket, clearly not empty—and he lowered his eyes at once. The man, on the other hand, was staring right at him.

"You're not from these parts, are you?" he asked. De Luca nodded, breathing heavily, his trench coat held close to his chest. He had to clear his throat before responding. He was so tense that even swallowing hurt.

"I'm just passing through . . . On my way from Bologna to Rome for work, but first I'm stopping in Ravenna, where I have relatives," he said hurriedly, as if he were reciting a poem. The man smiled.

"Dangerous place to be just passing through," the man said. "Full of land mines the Germans left behind. One little fellow lost his arm just yesterday. Can I see your papers?"

De Luca put his hand into his pocket so suddenly that the man reached towards his holster. He held his arm out stiffly and handed over his ID—a small rectangle of brand-new card, slightly creased on one side—together with a sheet of paper folded in four. The man took them and held them in his hand without looking down. He continued staring at De Luca. And smiling.

"Your name is?"

"Morandi," said De Luca, ready. "Morandi Giovanni, born—"

"Fine, fine. Morandi Giovanni . . . Fine . . ." He handed De Luca the papers, but when he went to take them, the man jerked his arm back and De Luca was left with his hand hanging in midair, embarrassed and confused beneath that flat gaze and that strange smile—a little slanted, drooping to one side. De Luca swallowed again and ran his tongue over his parched lips.

"And you are . . .?" he asked in a rush, his voice vibrating on the first word.

"Brigadier Leonardi," said the man. "Partisan Police. Where is it that I've seen you before, Signor Morandi? Milan? Have you ever been to Milan, sir?"

"I'm from Bologna," De Luca said.

"Milan, in '43 . . . Were you in Milan, in '43?"

"I'm from Bologna."

"Why, I'm sure it was . . . Yes, it was Milan all right, in '43 . . ."

Enough, thought De Luca. *That's enough, please. Leave me in peace . . .* Instead, he repeated: "I'm from Bologna." His words came out like a lament.

Leonardi looked away. He opened a pocket of his jacket and slipped the papers inside.

"Fine," he said. "Let's go." He turned and took a step forward.

De Luca didn't move.

"Let's go?" he asked, hoarse.

"I'll take you into town. In two hours it's going to be dark and you can't be wandering around like this at night. There are land mines and . . ." He looked straight into De Luca's eyes. "Somebody might mistake you for a fascist on the run. Every so often they come through here, trying to get south through the countryside. But they never make it. Trust me, Signor Morandi; let's head back to town. To avoid any mis-understandings." And he smiled again, oblique.

They followed the trail down to the road, where there was a jeep with an American star on the side, partly scraped away and covered by the letters CLN, in red. Leonardi climbed into the driver's seat, agile. De Luca sat beside him, wrapped up in his trench coat, shoulders hunched, his chin almost resting on his chest. He felt tired, so tired he kept his eyes closed, shut tight, and let himself be thrown around in that hard seat with every pothole they hit, not listening to Leonardi, who talked and talked, eyes glued to the road, talking all the while.

"I've been running the Sant'Alberto station," he said, "since right after Liberation. There's a lot to do, you know, because the area is pretty big and it's taken the carabinieri almost six months just to get back as far as San Bernardino. Sure, in theory I have two officers under me, but I prefer to do things myself. At times, though, a bit more experience . . ." He shot a sideways glance at De Luca, who didn't notice. "Because, well . . . you know what? I like this job. I really do."

Suddenly the jeep pulled up and De Luca opened his eyes. His heart was beating hard and the exhaustion he felt just minutes before disappeared at once. They were in the court-yard of a deserted farmhouse with barred windows.

"Why'd we stop here?" asked De Luca, straightening up in the seat. "This isn't town."

Leonardi jumped down from the jeep. "Have to do something," he said, calmly. "Come with me."

"Why?"

"I don't want to leave you here alone. It might start raining any minute now. Come inside with me." He approached De Luca and held out his arm, his other hand on his hip by the pistol. De Luca got out, avoiding contact, and followed him towards the house, trying to stay behind him, fear turning him so stiff he could hardly walk. He was breathing hard, audibly, through open lips, but Leonardi didn't seem to notice.

"A murder was committed here," said Leonardi, pointing towards the silent wall of the house. "A brutal murder. Four people and a dog." He indicated a chain attached to the wall that ran into the middle of the courtyard. At the end of the chain there was a dog collar, open, empty, like a gaping jaw. De Luca didn't look at it. He wasn't listening to a word Leonardi said. He was staring at the black grip of the pistol sticking out from under the man's jacket and moving with each step he took. Leonardi stopped in front of the door, pulled out a bunch of keys, chose one, and opened the door. He pushed it ajar with his foot and waved De Luca in.

"Please," he said.

De Luca clenched his teeth. He would have liked to scream, turn on his heels and run, but he was too afraid to think, so he just stepped forward—one long, awkward stride—and went into the dark room. He kept his eyes ahead of him, staring into the darkness, lacking even the courage to close them, and waited, his head spinning, his shoulders and neck muscles aching from tension, his hands clasped together inside the fabric of his trench coat. He waited. Waited. Waited.

When Leonardi opened a window, flooding the room with light, he let out a groan.

"The whole family beaten to death," said Leonardi, pacing the room.

De Luca watched him, dismayed. The pistol was still holstered.

"We found old man Guerra here." He stopped in front of a door and pointed to the floor. "He had one hand on the doorknob. Nearly had it open but they hit him over the head from behind. The young man, on the other hand, Delmo, head of the family, was here, on the ground, in the middle of the room." He stopped and opened his arms, tilting his head to one side, eyes wide open, his mouth agape. De Luca watched him. He didn't understand anything. The tension he'd felt earlier had left him drained and dazed. His legs were trembling slightly and he had to lean against a chair. Only then did he notice the large patches of dried blood on the floor. Even the walls were stained.

"He copped a beating, too," Leonardi continued. "But from the front. The old lady, on the other hand, was in the fireplace. There." He pointed to a fireplace with a chair overturned in front of it. "And as far as I'm concerned, she didn't even have time to move. Delmo's wife, meanwhile, was under the table. Here." He put his hand on the wooden table and crouched down to look beneath. "Yep, right here."

De Luca batted his eyelids, shaking his head.

"Why?" he said.

"Why what?"

"Why are you telling me this?"

Leonardi shrugged. "I'm thinking out loud. I'm conducting an investigation."

"Yes, but I . . . I'm not part of the investigation . . . I shouldn't be here. Police procedure—"

"Procedure?" Leonardi smiled, that strange crooked smile twisting his mouth. "You know something about police procedure, do you?"

De Luca shook his head, vigorously, turning sideways. "No," he said, firmly. "I thought . . . I just thought—"

"Right, you thought . . . Right." Leonardi began moving around the room again, frantic. "They were eating," he said, pointing to the table. "Not much, as you can see. Delmo was a petty thief and a small-time poacher; they lived off what he was able to bring home. This time, however, they didn't get the chance to finish their dinner. So, what do you think?"

"Me?" De Luca placed a finger on his chest. "Me?" he repeated.

"We're the only ones in this room."

"You think I did—"

"Of course not. Don't talk nonsense. I know you have nothing to do with it. Let's just say I'm asking you because I'm curious. So, what do you say about all this?"

"I say it's horrible."

Leonardi turned his eyes to the ceiling. "Good God," he muttered, irritated. "Fine, then, I'll tell you what I think. The Guerras were spending a quiet night at home. They were eating dinner. Right?"

De Luca shrugged. "Yes, I suppose so . . . I guess."

"Good. Then someone, someone who's got a beef with them, arrives, kills the dog and enters there." He pointed over his shoulder with his thumb. "Old man Guerra's door."

"Why there?" De Luca asked and immediately bit his lip.

"Because there's a window in there with a broken pane. I'll show you later. Okay, so they come in, unannounced, because Delmo was a suspicious type and he always kept his rifle within arm's reach. They jump the Guerras and beat them to death. Then they leave. Right so far?"

"Maybe . . . yes, sure." De Luca couldn't help glancing doubtfully towards the door, and his slight movement didn't escape Leonardi.

"What is it?"

"No, nothing . . ."

"Say it. By all means, say it."

"It's just that . . ." De Luca ran his hands over his stubbly chin, shaking his head. "Why would they kill the dog out front, and then come in through the back door?" He frowned, pursing his lips, thoughtful, and didn't notice the smile budding on Leonardi's lips. "And why . . . why, if they came in through that door, it sure is strange that the old man tried to make his escape there. And . . . Can I take a look?" He indicated the door and Leonardi hurried over and threw it open. The window in the next room had a perfectly round hole in it surrounded by shards of glass, like the outstretched fingers of an open hand.

"It was open," said Leonardi. "We closed it, but it was open."

De Luca nodded. He walked over to the window, opened it carefully so the glass wouldn't fall, and leaned out.

"No," he said. "No, I don't think so . . . There aren't any footprints outside, not even on the wall . . . This was already broken, and I'll tell you what, it almost seems as if . . ."

"Signor Commissario!" Leonardi said. De Luca turned mechanically.

"Yes?" he said firmly, and then pressed his lips together tightly. He closed his eyes as a shiver ran down his back, and when he opened them again Leonardi was looking at him, now smiling openly, satisfied—that damned smile of his! De Luca dropped his hands to his side, slumping, as if his arms had grown unbearably heavy.

"What do you want from me?" he said with a sigh.

CHAPTER TWO

"As far as I know, sir, you could be anybody; a bum, a professor, an engineer . . . There, let's just say you're an engineer. That okay with you?"

De Luca didn't say a word. He hadn't spoken since he'd climbed back into the jeep, his lips sealed, almost, shut. But Leonardi hadn't shut up for a single moment. He had taken De Luca into town and led him to an inn. The sign hanging next to the front door at least said it was an inn, but inside it looked like any other house. There were three wooden tables in the middle of the room and they sat down at the smallest of the three, De Luca immobile on the chair with his arms crossed and his lips sealed, and Leonardi leaning over the table towards him, elbows planted on the tabletop.

"Right, listen to me, Signor Engineer. You bear a striking resemblance to a certain Commissario De Luca, whom I met once when I was at a police-training course in Genoa. He was good, De Luca was. Everyone there considered him a legend . . . The academy's commander called him 'the most brilliant detective in the Italian police force.' Seems that later he lost his head a little with politics because now I come across his name again on a list of persons wanted by the CLN. Right up there with a lot of other bad names from the Social Republic, see? But let's leave Commissario De Luca out of this, let's leave him where he is." Leonardi turned towards a closed door. They were alone in the room, sitting before a large fireplace in which no fire burned, and it was getting dark because outside the sun was setting fast.

"So, is anybody here?!" Leonardi yelled at the door. Then he got up, opened the door and yelled again, "Is there anybody here?!" but he took a quick step back because a girl appeared in the doorway, bumping into him. Leonardi went back to the table.

"This is Francesca, Signor Engineer. Francesca, also known as la Tedeschina, the 'Little German.'" He went to grab her but without even looking at him she squirmed away, swinging her hips to avoid his reach. She went to get two glasses and a bottle from above the fireplace. Leonardi smiled.

"Just look how pretty our Francesca is. Don't you find that haircut of hers flattering?"

De Luca lifted his eyes and looked at the girl for the first time. She was very young and her black hair was short, cut in a strange way, uneven, like a boy's. It gave her a wild, brazen look, as did her eyes, which were also black. She stared at him with an intensity that was almost malicious.

"We call our Francesca 'la Tedeschina' because she was far too keen on the krauts," said Leonardi. "So she got herself a haircut compliments of the barber. Right, Tedeschina?"

"I went with the German because he was handsome," said the girl, tough, pouring wine into De Luca's glass. "And I go with whoever I like. Don't worry, you're not in any danger."

Leonardi smiled again then jumped suddenly to his feet, sending his chair backwards across the floor, because she had overfilled his glass, spilling wine on his trousers.

"Good God, Tedeschina!"

The girl glanced at De Luca, giving him a quick look that was like a smile, but a mean smile. She left the room clomping the soles of her clogs on the floor, covering Leonardi's voice as he cried, "Turn on the lights!" and leaving them in the dark.

"Electric light is the only reason this house rates as an inn, because la Tedeschina and her mother are the most backward individuals in all Romagna. Everybody knows that." Leonardi emptied his glass and immediately poured himself another. De Luca didn't drink. He was looking at the bottle, a half-liter bottle made of green glass with a bunch of grapes embossed in the centre of a hexagon with rounded angles. He recalled a similar one in his own home, when he was a child, and he would have liked to reach out and touch it but Leonardi started talking again.

"See, I like my profession. This work is in me, here," he said, touching his head with the tip of his finger. "And I think I'm good at it. But I need experience. I took a police-training course when the armistice was signed and I went straight off to the mountains, with the partisans . . . But the experience I've gained on my own isn't enough. It sure won't be enough before long because, you know, everything's about to change; there may well be a revolution in Italy, but the police—this much I've come to understand—the police force always stays the same. In Lugo they reorganized the precinct and then gave it back into the hands of the same people who were there before. And the mayor is a partisan! Trust me, a year from now they'll be sending us all back home, doesn't matter if Togliatti is in power or De Gasperi."

The lights came on suddenly, like lightening. De Luca even imagined he heard thunder, but it was only the clop-clop of la Tedeschina's clogs. She walked around the table carrying two plates brimming with some kind of red slop. She put one down in front of De Luca and dropped the other one in front of Leonardi, who once again had to jump back to avoid being splattered with tomato sauce. He reached out and this time managed to catch her as she went by.

"Come here a bit, you . . . Don't go running off like that all the time. What is this stuff?"

"Rabbit. Rabbit in red sauce." La Tedeschina had a tough

way with words, as if she always spoke with her chin up and her teeth clenched.

"Yeah? Rabbit, is it? This is a cat, I tell you."

"If you don't want it I'll take it back. And if you don't get your hands off my ass I'll tell Carnera."

Leonardi straightened up in his chair and the smile that was stretching his mouth wide crinkled slightly, just for a second.

"Get out of here!" he said. "The cat'll do. And you can keep your ass, too." He raised his hand to give her a slap on the behind as she walked away but then had second thoughts and was left with his arm hanging in midair in a kind of half-hearted Roman salute.

De Luca looked at the rabbit, the cat, or whatever it was, drowned in tomato sauce. He hadn't eaten since the evening before and he was hungry, but the warm stink of lard made his stomach tighten and close, and he felt dizzy and nauseous. Leonardi, on the other hand, had already polished off half his plate.

"You need references," he said with his mouth full. "Or, you show them you know how to get the job done. That's why I'm interested in the Guerras. This is the first case I've had that hasn't got anything to do with politics. Know what I mean? Nothing to do with politics . . . And it's a big deal. There, I want to solve it, I want to go to the carabinieri and tell them this happened and that happened, so-and-so did it and here, here's the evidence. But, like I said, I need experience. I need the help of . . . of an engineer. An engineer like you."

De Luca picked up his fork and prodded the meat, turning it over in the plate. His nausea had gotten worse and so had his hunger.

"Who's Carnera?" he asked, his voice hoarse after his long silence. He hadn't spoken in a good while.

"Carnera?" said Leonardi.

"That girl, la Tedeschina, said she'd tell Carnera if—"

Leonardi held up his hand and shook his head. "Right, you'd be better off leaving him be. Carnera has got real problems with . . . with engineers. He did the most incredible things during the war and he killed more Germans single-handedly than the whole Fifth American Army . . . He's a legend around here.

"But you're not answering me; you're trying to change the subject. So, Signor Engineer, are you going to help me with this case or not?"

De Luca pulled a piece of meat away from the bone but left it lying on the plate. He poured himself a glass of wine.

"Why," he said. "Do I have a choice?"

Leonardi smiled. "No, you don't."

The front door opened and two men came in. One of them, in shirtsleeves and wearing his beret slantwise, raised a hand to salute Leonardi. They sat down at the far table, but Leonardi leaned in toward De Luca anyway, moving the bottle aside to avoid bumping his nose.

"That whole thing about the window . . ." he whispered. "The broken glass and the fingerprints . . . I had figured it out, too. It was only to get you interested in the case."

"How do you know it's not political?"

"It's not political."

"How do you know?"

Leonardi sighed. "If it had been political, I would have heard something. I always hear something. And, the Guerras have never had anything to do with anything, not with the fascists, and not with us. Trust me, politics has got nothing to do with it. As far as I'm concerned, we're dealing with a robbery, people who came in to steal."

"Could be." De Luca gave the rabbit another try. He put a piece in his mouth, closed his eyes, and forced it down. "What does the coroner have to say?"

"The coroner?" Leonardi seemed surprised.

"A doctor, any doctor. You had a doctor look at them, right?"

"No. It's obvious they were beaten to death."

"Nothing is obvious in this line of work. How long did your course in Genoa last?"

Leonardi lowered his eyes. "Three months. Three months and that was it."

De Luca smiled, but felt immediately uneasy. He decided it was best not to insist and noticed that one of the two men was looking at him, staring. "It's called an autopsy," he said, like a professor. Leonardi nodded, moving his lips as he repeated the word. "Or a forensic medical examination, as you wish. Have they been buried already?"

"Tomorrow."

"Good. Find a doctor and have him examine them. Cause and time of death, any suspicious marks on the bodies, everything he can tell you. That's the first thing to do."

"The first thing to do," Leonardi repeated. De Luca skewered another piece of meat but his nausea outweighed his hunger and he let the fork fall on the plate. Leonardi didn't notice. His eyes were on De Luca but he seemed to be thinking of something else.

"I'll get on it right away. As for you, you'd better head off to bed. I want you shipshape tomorrow morning. Let's be sure we understand each other," he said, and he raised his hand and pointed his finger at De Luca, a finger as straight as the blade of a knife and just as threatening. "Outside this place, you're dead. Without documents you won't make it past the bridge, I guarantee it, not even if you had a patron saint watching over you. I'm your patron saint here, Signor Engineer. Don't forget it." He raised a hand to call la Tedeschina over but she looked away so he called another woman, a short woman with a kerchief on her head and an apron tied around her wide hips.

"Signore will be staying here for a few days," he said. "He's passing through and needs a rest. Take care of him. He's a friend of mine and a good man, an important man . . ." He stood and put his hand on De Luca's shoulder, squeezing it lightly. "A very important person. He's an engineer."

CHAPTER THREE

D e Luca woke with a start.

The night before, when he first set eyes on the bed—puffy, soft, and white, his first real bed in a week—he felt he could have collapsed there and then, his face sinking into the snow-white cushion. He managed to get undressed, and he slipped beneath the covers. But then, as usual, he slept badly, intermittently, curled up in the fetal position, his breathing stalling every now and again, and his brain refusing to switch off.

The sunlight filtering through the partially opened shutters struck his eyelids. In that brazen, luminous half-light what little sleep remained, weighing on his bones, left him. He sat up with a sigh, hanging his legs, inert, over the edge of the bed for a long while.

He rinsed his face in a basin and dried himself with a bed sheet, as he could find nothing else, then went downstairs. He had no idea of the time—he'd left his watch and its gold case with a guy in Milan in exchange for papers—but it must have been very early as the house was empty; even the kitchen, which was flooded by a calm, gray light. De Luca realized he was hungry—hungry and not nauseous, finally!—and he began looking around for something to eat. He tried to open the glass doors of a sideboard but they were locked. He tried the drawers underneath but they were empty. And that's how la Tedeschina found him when she came into the kitchen; on the floor, sly and embarrassed like a thief.

"There's nothing there," she said. "Mamma's got the keys to the pantry. But she's sleeping."

De Luca stood up, nodding his head. "I was hungry," he said. "I *am* hungry . . ."

La Tedeschina put down the bucket she was carrying, a metal bucket full to the brim with a mix of peas and dirt. "If you want," she said without any trace of politeness, "I can make you a coffee."

"Yes!" De Luca answered at once, almost yelling. "Yes," he repeated, quieter this time, and swallowed. La Tedeschina filled the caffettiera and lit the burner.

"You get up early," she said. "Why'd you become an engineer if you're gonna get up with the farmers?"

De Luca opened his arms wide. "I can't sleep anymore," he said, as if apologizing. She shrugged, didn't bother replying, and went to open the window, leaning out to latch the shutters. The sun burst violently into the room. But it was a gray, sickly sunlight, heavy with rain. She picked up a wooden chair and placed it in the middle of the bright patch of sunlight on the floor, then took a bowl, sat down, and placed the bowl in her lap and the metal bucket at her side. She slipped out of her clogs and put her heels up onto the wicker seat of a second chair. And with quick movements of her thumb she shucked the peas and emptied them into the dish, small and hard, like rifle shot. De Luca stood there watching her. He looked at her legs, smooth and young and straight between the two chairs, sticking out of short military pants she had rolled up over her thighs, and he felt ill, as if something was pushing from within, something soft and wet between his stomach and his heart, crushing him. La Tedeschina noticed and looked at him with those malicious eyes, a quick glance, from bottom to top. It was like being slashed with a knife.

"What are you up to, Engineer?" she said. "Looking at my

legs?" And with her short nails she scratched her knee, without malice, where there were signs of a recent scrape.

De Luca opened his mouth, blushed in embarrassment, held up his hands, and said, "I . . ." But just then steam began hissing from the caffettiera, spitting and sputtering from the spout. La Tedeschina stood up and handed him the bowl of peas. She turned the caffettiera over and filled a cup with coffee, then picked up the bowl again and returned to where she was as De Luca turned the coffee cup around in his hands so as not to burn himself. He took a sip immediately, unable to hold himself back: The sweet, bitter smell was stronger than anything; stronger than La Tedeschina's legs, stronger than the boiling liquid that burned his tongue. He stopped drinking only when the pain in his mouth got too much and tears began welling in his eyes.

"God . . ." he moaned. "It's been so long since I had real coffee . . ."

"We've always had coffee here," said la Tedeschina, settling herself in the chair. "We never went without, not even in winter, when the front was at the river."

De Luca blew on the coffee and gazed at her short irregular tufts of hair over the rim of his cup. He watched her in all innocence, but then she saw him looking at her and turned a violent red.

"I didn't go with the German for that," she hissed, buttoning her blouse, her thumb over the buttonhole. "I do whatever I please and nobody orders me around. Not even Carnera." The name emerged from between her tight lips like a growl, the *r*s loud and pronounced, hard. De Luca was about to ask her something when the door opened and Leonardi appeared in the doorway, tall, dark, silhouetted against the morning light outside.

"A good morning to you, Engineer. Shall we? We've got work to do."

*

"You know something? You were right." Leonardi was speaking a mile a minute; he was ecstatic, bouncing the jeep over holes in the road that ran alongside the river. Every now and again he turned towards De Luca, who was clinging to the dashboard grip. "You see what experience means? God, I still have so much to learn . . . I went to get the doctor last night. We went to the shack where I've been keeping the Guerras and I had him examine them thoroughly. I was right about the others, a belt in the head and goodnight. But not Delmo. No sirree. You were right: there was something else."

He turned towards De Luca and looked at him with an insistent smile, a smile that begged a question. He stayed that way until De Luca asked him the question, and in a damned hurry, because they were heading off the road.

"And what was it?"

"*What was it*? They didn't just kill poor Delmo, they tortured him."

"Tortured him?"

"Right, the whack on the head dazed him a little but he died later when his heart gave way under torture. Doctor said the marks on the body are clear as anything, no room for doubt. I'd seen marks like that before, too, when one of our boys came home dead from Bologna after being interrogated by the Black Brigade."

"Strange," said De Luca, but the roar of the motor covered his voice.

"You're probably wondering why I didn't see those marks in the first place," said Leonardi, and this time he didn't bother waiting for De Luca. "They weren't normal marks, like, I don't know, like on the hands or the feet . . . These marks were under his shirt, on his stomach muscles. With a knife, says the doctor. And it must have hurt like hell. Tomorrow he'll have a full report ready for me. What do you think? You think it's important?"

"Could be," said De Luca. "It depends. At first sight, it might look like someone was passing through, maybe someone from the Black Brigade looking for money or food. But I don't think so."

"Why not?"

"Precisely because he was tortured. Why bother torturing someone?"

Leonardi turned toward De Luca, who immediately guessed what he was going to say from Leonardi's sharp smile.

"Signor Engineer, if you don't know why they torture people, then I don't know who—"

De Luca squeezed his fists around the dashboard grip until his knuckles turned white.

"I have never tortured anyone," he hissed, stiffening. "Anyway, you torture somebody to get information from them. The Guerras lived in a poor house, that much is clear, and there's nothing suggesting hidden money or provisions stored away . . . In my opinion, the people that killed him were not passing through; they were people who knew exactly what they wanted to know."

"Locals, then . . . Perfect! This way, we're sure to get them."

De Luca smiled, shaking his head. "Sure to get them . . . And if we don't manage to solve the case? I do have a certain percentage of unsolved cases to my name . . . Not many, maybe, fewer than others, but a certain number nonetheless."

Leonardi nodded, convinced. "We'll solve the case, Engineer, we'll solve it. This is going to open the door to a brilliant future in the police force for me, and for you it's going to open the door to the possibility of having one at all, a future that is. What do you say, Engineer, shall we solve it?"

De Luca frowned gloomily. "We'll solve it," he said. "We'll have to."

The jeep came to a halt, stopping so suddenly that De Luca's entire weight fell on his arm. He felt a sharp pain in his wrist. Leonardi leaned out to the side and looked ahead, up along the road, which followed the embankment of the levee and disappeared around a bend. De Luca, sitting to his right, couldn't see anything beyond the bend.

"What is it?" he asked, but Leonardi simply lifted his arm. He looked worried.

"You stay here," he said, jumping out of the jeep. "Don't move and don't say a word."

De Luca nodded and settled back into the seat, his arms crossed over his chest, as Leonardi disappeared around the bend. He heard him talking to somebody and after a few seconds he came back. Leonardi got into the jeep and started the engine.

"Don't do anything," he whispered. "Don't move and keep your mouth shut. Look ahead, straight ahead, and that's it." His voice was glacial and gave De Luca reason to worry. As the car moved off he gazed ahead of him like a mannequin, his chin up and his neck muscles tight. But he couldn't help noticing, out of the corner of his eye, three men standing at the side of the road. And then he watched them vibrating in the rearview mirror: two with rifles, the other one a big man with a thin face and a prominent nose who was returning De Luca's gaze, examining *his* reflection in the rearview mirror. De Luca looked away immediately.

"Who were they?" he asked, with a touch of nervousness. "The big one's still staring at me."

"Forget you ever saw them, Engineer," said Leonardi, serious. "The big one was Carnera."

CHAPTER FOUR

"So, where do we start?"

Leonardi was on his feet in the middle of the room, rubbing his hands together, excited. De Luca was standing near the door, his hands deep in the pockets of his coat, a little hunched.

"We ought to be looking for clues, fingerprints, traces . . . Anything we can find."

"Okay, then, let's look for clues."

De Luca shrugged. "It's useless," he said. "You moved everything around, you've touched everything. That footprint there, in blood, for example, would seem to indicate that one of the killers was wearing American military boots, size forty-two, give or take."

Leonardi bit his lip, unconsciously dragging the sole of his boot across the floor.

"Right," he said. "I must have left it when I was carrying Guerra out. Christ, I've got so much to learn . . ."

De Luca looked around. There wasn't a thing in that farmhouse worth stealing, and yet . . . Four dead. Four dead to find something. But what? There were two floorboards sticking up in a corner of the room, and others further along, split in two. Leonardi was watching him, anxious, his mouth slightly open.

"We need a spade or some sort of iron bar," said De Luca. "And a knife."

"An iron bar?"

"To lift up the floorboards and check out the walls. The knife is for the mattresses. We'll start the search here."

"Right." Leonardi ran outside and came back in with the equipment. De Luca took the spade from him and together they started tapping on the floorboards, lifting up the loose ones. Then De Luca took the iron bar from Leonardi and started tapping the walls with it, carefully, knocking away the dirty plaster that clung to the bricks beneath. It took time to tap all the walls. After a while, Leonardi stopped and picked up the knife, doubt spreading over his face.

"But how do we know there's still something here to find?" he asked.

De Luca sighed. "We don't. But we're hoping that Guerra died before he talked and that whoever began the job was interrupted . . . or got tired of looking."

"Right," said Leonardi again. He disappeared through the doorway and De Luca heard the sharp sound of tearing fabric. He stopped tapping on the walls, turned old man Guerra's chair around in front of the fireplace and sat down, his chin cupped in his hands. Leonardi came back out of the room with the knife in his hand, like a murderer.

"Nothing," he said. "Not a damn thing."

"Leave things as they are," said De Luca. "It's useless with just the two of us. Whatever it is could be buried outside or in the doghouse . . ." De Luca closed his eyes and shrugged.

"Put your heart into it, Signor Engineer. Don't forget our agreement. Maybe it's here in the house, who knows, maybe in the soup cauldron . . ."

De Luca smiled, his eyes still closed.

"And what do you know, here is it is!"

De Luca opened his eyes and raised his head. Leonardi was on his knees in front of the fireplace, pulling his arm out of a blackened cauldron hanging beneath the flue. He walked over to the table holding something in his cupped hands, delicately, like a baby bird fallen from its nest. De Luca hesitated for a moment, then put his hands on his knees and stood up. He took two steps to the table and pushed Leonardi aside, almost brusquely.

"Let me see," De Luca said.

Leonardi took his hands away from a small bundle of fabric tied in a knot. He took a step back, looking on dutifully. De Luca had trouble untying the knot. When he finally did manage to open the piece of rag, Leonardi let out a whistle. There was a brooch with an enormous stone at its center and a gold clasp, a little twisted.

"So this is what they were looking for," said De Luca. "This Delmo must have been an eccentric millionaire."

Leonardi held the brooch up to the light and examined it. "And where the devil did this come from?"

"Maybe he was working the black market, or hiding someone who was in trouble."

"Delmo? For the love of God, no. Delmo wasn't in on anything, I told you. And to get ahold of something like this on the black market he'd have had to be selling oysters and caviar."

"Well, it sure isn't a family heirloom. At least not his family. I'd say he stole it from someone."

Leonardi frowned. De Luca sat back down, but then stood up again at once, his curiosity making him shake.

"Anyhow, it's on account of this brooch that he was tortured and killed. The first thing we have to do is find out where it comes from and how he ended up with it . . . Are there any rich families in this region?"

"Mmm . . ." Leonardi hesitated, at a loss. "Well, maybe one . . . the count's."

"Good," said De Luca firmly. "Let's pay the count a visit and ask him if this brooch is his."

"The count's not there anymore . . . He left. They say he

escaped to America because he was scared . . . You know, he was involved with the Germans. The only one left at the Villa is a maid."

"Doesn't matter. Maybe it's even better that way. Let's go see her."

"But she's old . . . Linina is in her seventies . . ."

De Luca looked at him sternly and Leonardi lowered his eyes. He weighed the brooch in the palm of his hand, biting his lip, and then shrugged.

"Fine, fine," he said. "Let's go see what Linina has to say."

They left the house. As Leonardi was closing the door, De Luca noticed something in the yard near the dog chain.

"What's that?" he said. He walked over to the collar lying open in the dust and kneeled down, Leonardi behind him, curious. There were several dark marks near the chain, black and heavy, like oil stains, and next to them, a straight, rectangular streak in the dust.

"You walked all around here too," said De Luca. "But these survived. What do you think?"

"A motorcycle."

"Good. This yours too?"

"No, I use the jeep. But I know whose it is. This is Pietrino's Guzzi. It leaves stains everywhere."

"Pietrino?"

"Pietrino Zauli. He lives nearby, and he knew the Guerras well."

"Good! Another element we can work with. This Pietrino of yours was here not long ago and maybe he'll be able to tell us something."

De Luca stood up and the effort made him a little dizzy. Leonardi frowned, his face growing dark.

"You think Pietrino might have—" he said.

"I don't think anything," said De Luca. "It's not time yet to be thinking. Let's go visit Linina before it starts raining."

*

The rain caught them by surprise when they were halfway down the road. The only warning was a rapid change in light and the strong, wet odor of steel. A violent cloudburst with large heavy raindrops sent them running and the villa appeared so suddenly and unexpectedly amidst the trees at the end of the road that both men stopped in their tracks for a moment before taking cover beneath the balcony that hung over the front door.

"Good God," said Leonardi. "I'm soaked! But we did need a bit of rain, for the countryside."

De Luca stared at him grimly, not saying a word. He pulled his trench coat tight around his neck, with a shiver because the rain was slipping through his hair and running down his back, an awful sensation that was driving him crazy.

"Let's go inside," he yelled over the noise. The rain was getting even heavier. He made for the door, but Leonardi stopped him, putting his hand on De Luca's arm.

"This is a strange house, Signor Engineer," he said. "It's a house where you *feel things*."

"You feel things?"

"Yes, what is it you say round your parts? There are spirits."

De Luca shivered, mostly because of the way Leonardi pronounced that word, *spirits,* serious and worried.

"What nonsense," he said, shrugging and giving the door a shove. The door opened immediately and they stepped inside. Inside, due to some strange acoustic effect, the rain was barely audible, even though it continued to whip across the ground behind them, violent and very close. De Luca shivered once more.

"Anybody here?" he said, then repeated more loudly, "Anybody here?" There was no answer. He entered a long, empty corridor and opened a door, but there, too, he found an empty room with high ceilings and no furniture, and his voice echoed when he again called out, "Is there anybody here?" making him draw his head down between his shoulders.

"Hey, Engineer! Wait a second," said Leonardi, holding him by his trench coat. "Are we going in just like that, alone?"

De Luca jerked himself free of Leonardi. "Police, Leonardi," he said with a harsh tone in his voice. "The police go wherever they want."

They crossed the room, their footsteps echoing in the cold silence, and came to a staircase leading to the floor above. De Luca hesitated for a moment, leaning on the wooden railing, because he recalled a dream that he always had when he was a child. There was a staircase, like this one, and he climbed and climbed right to the top, without, however, noticing her standing there: an old hunchbacked woman waiting for him, smiling . . .

"What nonsense," said De Luca aloud, and as Leonardi was asking, "What'd you say, Engineer?" he began climbing the stairs, resolute.

At the top of the stairs was another closed door. De Luca opened it expecting to find another empty room, but instead he stood in the doorway to a small room jammed with furniture, so full it seemed impossible to enter. He didn't realize somebody was there until the somebody moved, between a chair and an armchair. It was an old hunchbacked woman, dressed in black, like in the dream.

"Have you come for the furniture, too?" she said. De Luca was frozen with his mouth open and couldn't get an answer out. Leonardi stepped forward, slipping between De Luca and the doorframe, and went into the room.

"Oh," said the old woman. "Aren't you Marietto's son?"

"This is Linina, Engineer," said Leonardi. "The count's maid. Talk up because she's a bit deaf."

The woman came towards De Luca, looking up into his face. "Why, isn't this Gigetto's son?" she asked Leonardi, then she moved across the room, fast, though dragging her feet, and took a doily off one of the chairs. "Take this," she said. "It's still good . . . Take whatever you need, it's of no use here, just collects dust. I'm too old and ever since they took the young master away . . ."

"The count is gone, Linina," interrupted Leonardi. "He went to America."

The woman shrugged her shoulders draped in a black shawl, then turned to face De Luca. "How are you, Gigetto?"

De Luca came to his senses. "Fine," he said quickly. He gestured to Leonardi, who took his hand from his pocket, holding the brooch.

"We wanted to show you something, Linina," he said, opening his hand. "Do you recognize this? Did it belong to the count?"

The woman squinted, her nose almost touching Leonardi's palm, then smiled.

"Oh, there it is, finally! Well done!" she said and fast as anything she snatched the brooch from Leonardi's hand before he was able to close it and put it away in a drawer. De Luca nodded.

"It belonged to the count," she said. Leonardi opened the drawer and took out the brooch, gently pushing the woman's hands back.

"We'll hold onto this, Linina, it'll be better that way. Right, well, I think we've sorted everything out . . . We can go." Leonardi turned to go, but De Luca didn't move.

"Just a minute," he said. "I'd like to ask the Signora another question . . . Can you recall when the brooch went missing? When, that is, did you notice that . . . ?"

"Why, when the ring disappeared."

"The ring?"

"The blue ring that went with the brooch. They were a set . . . Why? You didn't take them, did you?"

"And the ring, when did the ring go missing?"

De Luca expected her to reply, "When the brooch went missing," but instead the woman creased her brow, as if contemplating the question, and then shrugged.

"When the young master went missing," she said. "When he disappeared to America."

De Luca nodded and glanced at Leonardi.

"And when the count left for vacation, what happened exactly? Did someone drop by? Was it daytime or evening?"

"It was in the evening, because I had just fed the dogs . . . The young master was in his room with Sissi—a grand eater, Sissi . . . That's when those men arrived and told me to stay in the kitchen. When I came out the young master was gone and so was Sissi."

De Luca nodded. "Seems like they've got a thing about killing dogs," he said.

"The count is gone," Leonardi said. "He went to America."

De Luca nodded again. "All right, all right," he said. "One more thing: those men? Do you remember who they were?"

"Oh . . ." The woman opened her arms, her thin lips twisted into a grimace. "I'm an old woman and I can't remember things . . . I remember the son of that fellow next door to the shoemaker's . . ." She turned to face Leonardi. "Baroncini, the short one . . . but then, you know, you were there, too."

"Me?" said Leonardi, glancing at De Luca, who was staring back at him. "Me? No, you're wrong, I . . ."

Just then the lights came on, making them jump. De Luca instinctively looked up.

"The young master doesn't like to be in the dark," said the woman.

"Nonsense," De Luca said. "It's the storm."

"Let's go," said Leonardi. "Let's go, please."

"It's not what you think, Engineer."

"I don't think anything at all."

It had stopped raining and a damp sticky heat that was almost worse than the storm was rising out of the wet earth. De Luca had taken his trench coat off and was doing his best to stay on his feet as he walked down the muddy drive. Leonardi forged ahead, fearlessly stomping through the sludge in his military boots, but De Luca, with his low-cut shoes beginning to come apart at the seams, had to be careful not to slip with every step.

"Old Lina is a little, how should I put it . . ." Leonardi waved his hand in front of his forehead. "A little . . . feeble-minded."

"She seemed perfectly lucid to me."

Leonardi stopped and grabbed De Luca's arm, forcing him to turn and reach for Leonardi to stop from falling.

"Listen to me, Signor Engineer," he said brusquely. "I don't know anything about any of this . . . I wasn't in charge at the time, I was just a police officer . . . But why am I explaining myself to you? What do you want from me?"

"Me? I don't want anything, heaven forbid . . . Seems to me you're the one who wanted to solve this case."

"Yeah, that's right, the Guerra case, not the count's."

"Guerra was killed because of a brooch. The brooch belonged to the count. The two cases are connected."

"Shit." Leonardi took one step, like he was about to walk off, but then stopped suddenly. He leant back against a tree and put his hands in the pockets of his jacket.

"It's a strange story," he said, lost in thought, looking down at the ground. "You see, Engineer, around here, after the war, there were lots of stories like this one . . . People who deserved what they had coming, things that simply had to be done . . . But, well . . . I already told you: I'm not interested in hearing the opinions of people like you."

De Luca sighed, lifting his eyes up to the heavens.

"But this story . . ." continued Leonardi, "the count's story is something altogether different. Don't get me wrong, the count deserved what he got, and how! He was a goddamned son of a bitch. He was a spy for the Germans, he told them that there were weapons stored in a farmhouse and they shot an entire family, women and children included. And he was a pervert, he offered hospitality to the SS, and they say he even took some of them to bed. It's amazing they didn't get rid of him earlier." Leonardi shook his head slowly and wet his lips with his tongue. "But that's beside the point . . . The strange thing is that while everyone knew something, at least something, about the other things that happened, nobody said a word about this afterward, or even during. No, not a word, not even amongst us."

"That's strange?"

"It's strange, all right . . . I was here that night, but I only know what I saw; not much. It was May, the seventh of May I think, and it must have been around nine when I got to the villa to impose the curfew on the count—"

"The curfew?"

"Yes, to tell him that he couldn't leave the house until morning . . . That's how we do things with suspicious types. Anyhow, on the way back I saw Pietrino, with his motorbike, heading in the direction of the villa. Behind him, on the seat, was Sangiorgi, who was my chief at the time."

"And?"

"And nothing. I went back to town and the next morning I heard that the count had disappeared. Gone to America. Why are you looking at me like that?"

"I'm not looking at you. I'm waiting."

"Waiting for what?"

"Your decision."

Leonardi pushed himself away from the tree and pulled his hands out of his pockets. "Couldn't we just forget about this whole thing?" he asked.

De Luca grimaced.

"Perhaps. Who knows? But the Guerras were killed because of a brooch . . ."

"And the brooch belonged to the count, I know. Good God, Engineer, why the devil did we chose this line of work? Do you have any idea why?"

De Luca smiled. "Because we're curious," he said. Leonardi raised an eyebrow, puzzled, then shrugged.

"Well," he muttered. "I suppose we could have a chat with Sangiorgi, after all. You know, a friendly chat . . ."

CHAPTER FIVE

Sangiorgi was a small man with a nervous air about him. His hair was completely white though he still seemed young and was shoveling lime into a wheelbarrow, knocking the shovel against the edge of the barrow to free it of dust with every load. Leonardi had to call his name twice to make himself heard over the noise of the furnace and the short, sharp clangs of the shovel against the wheelbarrow.

"Hey, Guido," said Sangiorgi. He planted the shovel in the middle of the barrow, loosened a kerchief that was tied around his neck and used it to wipe the sweat from his face. He pointed in the direction of a shack, in front of which was a chair; hanging from the back of the chair was a straw bag, and sticking out of the bag was the neck of a bottle. "Doesn't matter, anyway," he said, "even if I do take a breather. I haven't got any sacks for the lime. I got the lime but I haven't got the sacks. One barrow load at a time! Is this any way to work?"

He pulled the bottle from the bag and poured a mouthful of wine into a glass, swished it around with a flick of his wrist to wash out the glass, and then poured it onto the ground and refilled the glass halfway. He offered it to Leonardi, who pointed to De Luca.

"First the engineer," he said.

"Oh, my apologies. An engineer, eh? Did you see my furnace? How does it strike you?"

"Nice work," De Luca said, covering his mouth immediately with the glass, as he didn't know what else to say.

"It's one of the few things that survived the war, but we're short just about everything else. The bombs destroyed half the town and the Germans carried away the other half. What survived, by miracle, what little survived, I might add, was taken by the Poles . . . like the burlap sacks. Here's hoping they meet with an accident. Let me have a drink, Engineer, otherwise I get angry and my blood pressure hits the roof."

He poured himself a glass of wine as De Luca slapped a hand over his stomach. A sharp, sudden pain made him clench his teeth. Leonardi didn't notice anything; he waited until Sangiorgi had finished drinking and took the glass from him.

"I wanted to ask you something," he said, distractedly, as if what he had to say wasn't really important. "Something about the count."

"That murdering lowlife of a count," Sangiorgi said, serious. Leonardi nodded.

"Yeah, sure, he was a pig, and a fascist . . . But I wanted to ask you something. Tell me about that night. What happened?"

Sangiorgi glanced at De Luca, then he turned to Leonardi, who was smiling, relaxed.

"Well? Aren't you going to pour me some wine?"

"I don't know. I ain't sure if I'm giving you anything to drink or not. What's up, Guido, you trying to fuck me over?"

Leonardi shook his head. He put his hand on the neck of the bottle and tilted it down towards the glass.

"You know me," he said. "We've been in the shit together, haven't we? Don't you remember? A whole week stuck in that shelter, Germans all around us . . . And who was it that carried you back when you broke your leg?"

Sangiorgi sighed, a quick sigh that emerged between his lips like a whine.

"Yeah, yeah. I know. But what about him? I know you all right, but not this fellow here . . ."

Leonardi put his hand on De Luca's shoulder and gave it a shake. De Luca, who was not expecting it, lost his balance, stepping to the side so as not to fall.

"I know the good engineer. You can trust him, Sangio. I'll vouch for him. Whatever you say will be kept between us."

"Christ Almighty, Guido," muttered Sangiorgi. "What kind of stories are you digging up now?" He sat down on the chair, bottle in one hand and glass in the other. "Anyway, I don't know anything either. It wasn't like the other times. At first, yeah, we went there with a motorcycle and the car, a Topolino, to haul off that bastard of a spy, but then . . . then, something happened."

"Who was there?" asked De Luca and Leonardi looked at him quickly and seriously, but Sangiorgi continued talking, shaking his head as he did so.

"The usual crowd. Me and Pietrino on the bike. And Carnera, of course."

De Luca opened his mouth to speak but Leonardi squeezed his arm, hard, almost hurting him.

"Pietrino locked Linina in the kitchen, downstairs," continued Sangiorgi. "And I went to check on the dogs. Carnera didn't need me; he was big enough to bring the count down alone. But then, out of the blue, Carnera comes down and tells us to leave. What're you talking about, I say, we have to wait for the truck so we can load up the stuff that we need in town. And he says no, come back tomorrow with the truck. Get Pietrino, get on the motorcycle, and get out of here. You know what Carnera's like when he's giving orders; you got to follow them. So we left, and I don't hear anything more about it."

"And you didn't ask anyone about what happened?"

Sangiorgi lifted his eyes to De Luca's, a cruel grin on his face.

"Why? I suppose *you* did, eh? Anyway, the answer's yes, I tried. The next day I asked Pietrino and he told me that worrying yourself about certain facts can get you a bullet in the head. And I said, 'Evening, thanks very much, and all the very best.'" He poured himself another glass of wine, held the glass up as if he were making a toast and emptied it in a single gulp. De Luca waved Leonardi over.

"What's this story about the truck?" he whispered. Sangiorgi heard him and jumped to his feet.

"Why?" he said. "Has somebody been complaining? We did things the same as always . . . Ask Piera, she's got all the records down at section headquarters."

Leonardi put his hands up in front of him, nodding. "Of course, of course, nobody's got any doubts about you. It's just that the engineer isn't familiar with certain practices. You see, the assets belonging to fascists who have been put to death are given out to needy families as kind of compensation for war damages. There is a special committee for this very purpose, and Sangiorgi is the chairman."

"Which means we know who got the brooch."

Leonardi snapped his fingers. "Sure we do," he said and turned to Sangiorgi, but he froze the minute he saw the latter's puzzled expression.

"What brooch?" asked Sangiorgi.

"The count's brooch . . ."

"There wasn't any brooch."

De Luca looked at Leonardi. He was staring at Sangiorgi, pale.

"There were two wardrobes, a few rifles, some money and some books that went to the library, but no brooch."

"You're sure?" De Luca asked. Sangiorgi straightened up and stuck his chin out in an aggressive way. It almost seemed as if he was standing on the tips of his toes.

"Of course I'm sure!" he said. Leonardi put his arm out in front of De Luca, as if he wanted to keep the two men apart.

"Okay, Sangio, okay . . . Everything's fine. We made a mistake. Let's go, Engineer . . ." He pushed De Luca away, but he wouldn't go.

"Just a second," he said. "There's one missing, the one the maid saw . . . He hasn't said a word about him."

"Right, Baroncini . . . Listen, Sangio, where was Baroncini?"

Sangiorgi shrugged. "Who the hell knows? He wasn't with us . . . Carnera has never wanted him in his GAP, and rightly so, because he was a bastard. But you might go saying that I'm just jealous, because he's got two new trucks and here I am filling a wheelbarrow." He put the cork back into the bottle and slipped both bottle and glass back into the straw bag, then he gestured to a man who was waiting by the wheelbarrow with a bucket in his hands and walked off. But he stopped after two steps and turned towards Leonardi.

"Do me a favor, Guido, a big favor. Don't come around here no more."

Sitting behind the steering wheel, his lips pressed tight, and his eyebrows knotted, Leonardi was staring at something on the hood of the jeep. De Luca, on the other hand, was staring up into space, running his hand over his chin, utterly absorbed as if he were listening to the sound his fingers made as they ran over his stubbly skin. Suddenly, Leonardi raised his arm and slammed his fist down on the steering wheel. De Luca jumped.

"What is it?" he asked, alarmed.

"Nothing, nothing . . . personal problems." Leonardi leaned down and touched the keys, but then, without starting the engine, he straightened up again. "This isn't good, Engineer, this isn't good at all . . . This story is getting way too complicated. And to think it looked like a simple robbery. Jesus, Mary, and Joseph!"

"Essentially, it is exactly that," said De Luca, to himself, following the thread of a thought. "The Guerras were killed for that brooch. To be precise, Delmo was tortured and killed for the brooch and the others merely because they were there with him at the time. Now, the question is, where did that brooch come from? This Carnera fellow . . ."

"Forget about Carnera, Engineer. I've already told you once."

"Fine, so let's forget about Carnera . . . but the other one, Pietrino—"

"Forget Pietrino too, Engineer."

"Forget Pietrino . . . All right, then it probably happened like this: one morning Delmo wakes up and realizes that the tooth fairy has put a marvelous brooch under his pillow . . ."

"Oh, please!"

"*Oh, please* . . . How do you plan to solve this case if you eliminate all the suspects? Brigadier Leonardi, that brooch never arrived at the committee premises because someone slipped it into their pocket!"

"Shit!" said Leonardi, once more bringing his fist down on the steering wheel, this time so hard that his hand slipped off to the side and he cut himself on the dashboard.

"I agree with you Brigadier. Wholeheartedly," muttered De Luca. He continued looking at Leonardi, who was sucking his injured hand. Then he said, "So?"

"So what?"

"Do you intend to continue with this investigation? If you want to hand the carabinieri something concrete . . ."

Leonardi looked to his side, his face dark and malicious.

"No matter what, I've always got something I can hand over to the carabinieri," he said and started the engine, leaving De Luca speechless and frozen in his seat.

CHAPTER SIX

He spent the whole day inside his room at the inn, lying on the bed, intent on the beveled roof beams, his arms extended at his sides, immobile. Every so often, one of the thoughts spinning around in his head came to a standstill, grabbed on to some more tangible detail, and struggled to get to the surface, making his heart race. In those moments, he shut his eyes tight, shook his head, sat up on the edge of the bed with his face in his hands, or got up and pressed his forehead against the windowpanes, avoiding looking out, and he felt like hurling the water basin against the wall and kicking the door to pieces. But then, as soon as it passed, he stretched back out on the bed and began studying the ceiling again. As a child, when a sudden creak filled the darkness of the bedroom with nightmares readying to pounce, all you had to do was pull the sheets up over your ears and wait, your eyes shut tight, until dawn when the sun, brightening the windows, brought with it an exhausted and liberating sleep that lingered until Mamma arrived with warm milk and then school. But what if it had really happened? What if some rapacious claw had suddenly pulled back the sheets, hurling him back into the darkness, or a heavy hand had crushed him in his bed, murdered by sleep monsters . . . De Luca pressed his eyes shut, tight, shaking his head violently on the pillow; fear was coursing through his stomach again, with a sharp, intense, cold shiver, leaving room for nothing else.

A little earlier, or a lot earlier—without a watch he was never able to keep track of time—he'd been thinking that maybe it was better just to get everything over and done with quick—Leonardi and his crooked smile, the carabinieri—or worse, to put an end to this absurd situation of being a prisoner, incognito, immobile and impotent. But then someone knocked at the door and he clenched his jaw, frozen in terror, his heart beating like mad, though it turned out to be la Tedeschina only, asking him if he was coming down to eat something. He couldn't even answer her, nor move, until a dry heave from his empty stomach sent him running to the basin, futilely opening his mouth wide over the stagnant water.

It was almost evening when he went downstairs. He thought he'd find the room with the fireplace empty as it had been the day before, with that calm, reassuring half-light, but instead he was surprised, frozen in the doorway: all the tables were taken and the room was full of people, of smoke and a dense buzz which he noticed now for the first time. He hesitated, embarrassed, at the door, unsure if he should simply turn around and leave. But they had already noticed him and some of them had turned to stare at him. La Tedeschina's mother took care off things: on her way past him, she pushed him rudely into the room from behind.

"Oh," said a man wearing glasses, pointing at him. "He must be the engineer!"

De Luca glanced over his shoulder, furtively, but the man was already on his feet, placing another chair at the corner of the table for De Luca.

"Please, take a seat with us, Engineer, we're having a drink among friends in honor of Carlino, who's just returned from Russia today!"

De Luca shook the man's hand and sat down, mumbling, "Pleased to meet you," his eyes lowered, at every name he heard.

"Veniero Bedeschi, president of ANPI, the Italian National Association of Partisans, Sant'Alberto chapter, Meo Ravaglia, Franco Ricci, Carlino . . . and Learco Padovani, known as Carnera."

De Luca looked up, brusquely, and only then realized that right in front of him, at the other end of the table, sat the same big man with the thin face and the aquiline nose that he had seen that morning. He was staring at De Luca, the same stare that he had seen reflected in the rearview mirror of the jeep, the same black eyes, insistent and cruel, like la Tedeschina's. De Luca shivered.

"You know, I studied engineering at university, too," said the man with the glasses, Savioli or Saviotti, who had introduced himself as the mayor, or so De Luca thought. "I wanted to specialize in railroads, civil engineering, but then the war came along, and the Resistance, and I had to interrupt my studies. Are you a civil engineer, too?"

"No, mechanical," said De Luca, evasive.

"Oh, what a shame. I would have liked to talk about—"

"What are you doing around these parts?" interrupted Carnera. He had a deep, clipped, distinct voice, the kind that immediately overwhelms others. De Luca hid his hands under the table so they wouldn't see he was nervous.

"I'm passing through," he said. "I come from Bologna and I'm stopping here for while to—"

"Passing through, heading where?"

"Rimini, then Rome. I've got a job that—"

"Why didn't you take the train?"

"Ah, because I—"

"Learco, listen—" The mayor attempted to intervene, but Carnera didn't even look at him.

"Have you got papers?"

"Well, I—"

"Learco—"

"Show me your papers."

"Learco, Good God!" Bedeschi, the president of the ANPI, abruptly put his hand up. "Guido's in charge of the police station! Let him take care of these things!"

Carnera didn't say a word, but he didn't take his eyes off De Luca, who was trying to smile, uncomfortable. To get a grip on himself he picked up a glass of red wine that another man sitting nearby had poured for him.

"Hey, Engineer," said Savioli, or Saviotti. "You oughta come work here. Forget about Rome! Here there's more than enough to do. The front came to a standstill down at the river, and for two months we copped cannon fire from all sides, the Germans, the English, the Poles. There were practically no windows left in the whole town. But we got straight to work . . . Have you seen our schoolhouse, Engineer? We're rebuilding it by ourselves, with the money we get from the cooperative."

"Is that so?" said De Luca, with exaggerated interest. But Carnera was still staring at him from the other end of the table, and De Luca felt it, even though he didn't look in his direction, he could see him out of the corner of his eye, leaning heavily on the tabletop, his enormous hands resting on his arms, his wide shoulders and his thick neck, his thin, chiseled, swarthy face. Under the table De Luca was clenching his hands so tight it hurt.

"And this is only the beginning, Signor Engineer," said Bedeschi. His hair was gray and he sported a thin moustache that ran flush with his upper lip. "A year from now, Sant'Alberto will be better than ever. You know why? Because we're all of one mind here. I don't know what your politics are, Engineer—"

"No. I'm not interested in politics," said De Luca hurriedly. Bedeschi nodded, serious.

"Neither am I, if by politics you mean idle talk and nothing more. But when politics means planning the future, well, the time is right. The fascists and the Germans have been given their marching orders and now it's time for us to rebuild. Don't you agree, Engineer?"

De Luca shrugged, embarrassed. "Well, now . . . I—" he said before Carnera's deep voice drowned his out and pierced the indistinct murmur circulating in the room.

"Good riddance to the fascists, good riddance to the Germans, and well done, boys! Now it's all over we can all go back home. What's your word for it, Savioli? *Normalization . . .*"

"The war's over, Learco," said the mayor, harsh, his voice shaking.

"Ah, it's over, is it? I didn't notice, because frankly I see the same people around as before, here and in Rome, the same scheming sons of bitches, the same braying sons of the cloth. Certain talk is only possible in thickheaded company like this!" and he hammered his closed fist against the forehead of the man sitting next to him, staring at the mayor, who instinctively pulled his head back.

"Things are going to change, Learco," said Bedeschi, with an indulgent smile. "You'll see, they'll change, and quickly too . . . but you've got to have the right system."

"I've got a system." Carnera slapped his hand against his coat, near his belt. "And I been relying on it all right for some time now."

The mayor pulled out a newspaper folded lengthways and held it up, waving it as he spoke.

"In today's *L'Unità*," he said, "there's a column by Togliatti where he says, 'We want a democratic nation, a strong, well-ordered nation with a single army and a single police force . . .'"

Carnera pushed himself up onto his feet, tore the newspaper from the mayor's hand, and threw it violently down on the table. De Luca grabbed it mid-flight, right before it knocked over a glass.

"Bring Togliatti here!" roared Carnera. "I got something I'd like to say to dear Palmiro! If he really wants my gun, well here it is! Come and get it!" He reached under his coat, drew his revolver, and slammed it down on the table.

"Talking with you is impossible!" hissed the mayor, sitting back stiffly in his chair. De Luca swallowed, uneasy. Things were heating up and despite the fact that Bedeschi was waving his hands around and smiling, De Luca was scared. He would have liked to get up and leave, but that wasn't possible. Instead, he opened the paper and began to read, letting his eyes skim over the bold, black headlines, acting like he was engrossed in the news. "CLN Congress Closes: Northern Italy Favors a Republican Constitutional Convention," and further down, "Today At 3:30 in Tokyo Bay, Signing of the Japanese Surrender" and "Seven November: A Report by Vasco Pratolini. Italian prisoners begin returning from Russia, The people rejoice . . ." He turned the page, stopping at the headline, "Crime of Jealousy: Smashes Husband's Skull in with an Iron Bar," and was actually about to read the article, curious, when a short piece way down on the left, all on its own, attracted his attention. He had read the headline in its entirety before his brain managed to unpack the meaning of the words. FASCIST EXECUTIONER ARRESTED, said the large letters, and underneath in italics, "*Captain Rassetto recognized in Pavia. How many more criminals formerly of the Political Squad are still in hiding?*"

De Luca closed the newspaper quickly, tearing the page. Carnera stopped talking and raised his eyes to De Luca. Bedeschi put his hand on the other man's arm.

"What's the matter, Engineer? Are you feeling all right? You look pale . . ."

"It's nothing," said De Luca. "It's the heavy air, the heat . . ."

"Drink a glass of wine, then."

They poured him a glass of red wine, and though he shook his head he had to drink it, with Carlino pushing his elbow up making sure he finished it down to the last drop. Carnera smiled, staring at him. He leaned across the table and poured him another glass and when De Luca tried to push the glass away, he filled all the other glasses and held his up.

"To the people," he said. De Luca repeated the same words, "To the people," with the others, and drank. The minute he put the glass down on the table it was full again.

"To progress," said the mayor and De Luca repeated, "To progress." His glass was full again in a flash.

"To Carlino, back from Russia," said Bedeschi.

"To Carlino, of course!"

"Your turn, Engineer," said Carnera, handing him the bottle. "Give us a toast, won't you? C'mon, let's hear it!"

De Luca took the bottle from Carnera, but his hand slipped on the glass and he only avoided dropping it by tightening his hold around its neck. His head was spinning. The murmur in the room had gotten stronger, almost intolerable, and the smoke was like a thick fog that clouded everything. Carnera was staring at him, from far away, those mean eyes planted in his.

"To good health," De Luca managed.

They weren't quick enough to grab him. He fell backwards, knocking his chair over.

A sharp pain woke him up, like a club on the head, reverberating between his ears and making him open his eyes, with the distinct feeling of being covered in blood. But instead he was sitting on the bed, unhurt, with la Tedeschina trying to prop him up.

"If you keep coming a cropper like that, Engineer, you'll split your head open one of these days. Why drink if you can't hold it?"

"Oh God," mumbled De Luca. He closed his eyes, bending his chin down to his chest, but she lifted his head up brusquely.

"Sit up, Engineer, else how am I gonna get your shirt off? You want to go to bed in your clothes?"

De Luca lifted his chin, as docile as a child, and resisted the solicitations of those fingers moving rapidly around his neck. La Tedeschina unbuttoned his shirt, with effort, pulled it out of his pants, and then tried to get him to hold his arms up so she could pull the sleeves up over them, but he lost his balance and fell backwards across the bed.

"Well done," she said, roughly. "Stay right there, then, and good night."

De Luca heard the sound of her clogs moving away from him and tried to sit up. He didn't want to stay there alone, his head bent backwards, in a room that was spinning.

"Francesca," he muttered. "Francesca . . ."

The door, which had just closed, reopened. Francesca got up onto the bed, on her knees, with a sigh. She pulled and pulled until she managed to get one sleeve free, then she lifted her eyes and saw her reflection in the wardrobe mirror.

"Oh, look!" she said, surprised, a childish surprise that made her smile, this time a genuine smile. De Luca, too, lifted his head and saw himself in the mirror, a stubbly, pallid face, disheveled, popeyed like an owl. La Tedeschina arched her back, pulling her blouse tight over her side and lifted her chin, watching herself in the mirror all the while, turning her head to one side and then the other.

"You're beautiful," said De Luca, without malice. She shrugged, touching her short hair. "You're beautiful anyway," he said. "Even like that."

She looked at him, indifferent, and he felt embarrassed, half drunk and half dressed, ridiculous. He tried to remove his shirt altogether, but his entire weight was resting on the wrong elbow. La Tedeschina smiled. She bent over him, passing her arm behind him, lifted him up and pulled the other sleeve free. De Luca inhaled the warm, strong and slightly tart smell rising from under her shirt. He shivered and sighed. She noticed.

"It don't look to me like you're up to certain things," she said, cruelly. "And if Carnera finds out he'll kill you."

"Enough of this Carnera!"

De Luca raised himself up, the effort making him breathe heavily. He dragged himself up the bed toward the pillow, finally leaning his shoulders against the wooden headboard. She remained at a distance, watching him, propped up on one arm with her knees bent, swinging her legs.

"He didn't want me in here with you," she said. "He carried you up when you collapsed, he threw you on the bed and then he closed the door. But I came up anyway."

"Thanks. And why did you come back?"

La Tedeschina shrugged. "Because I did, that's all. I do whatever I want. And with whoever I want."

"Even with Germans."

"Who I happen to like, yes. Nobody's ever bought me, mister. He gave me a present once . . ."

"The German?"

She stretched out her leg and gave him a shove, hard, with her foot. "No, not the German, Carnera. But I threw it in the river. I don't want commitments. I'm free."

"Good for you, Francesca," De Luca sighed, tired, his head falling back against the headboard. "Good for you, Tedeschina. At least you know what you want. I, on the other hand, I don't know anymore. I don't know anything anymore. I don't even know if I'll be alive tomorrow." He closed his eyes and thought that maybe, just maybe, he might be able to fall asleep. But then she moved, making the bed sheet rustle, and came towards him, very near, near enough that he could feel her breath, cool, on his ear.

"Go away, please," he murmured, burying the side of his head against his shoulder so he wouldn't feel her intermittent solicitation that sent a tight shiver down his back.

"I do what I like," said la Tedeschina. She touched his chest with her open hand, a cold and rough caress that moved down over his stomach and made him breathe heavily and tremble, as if he had a fever.

"Please," he sighed, his eyes shut. "Please, Francesca, please . . . I'm dirty, tired, and desperate. I haven't eaten in two days and I'm shaking like a leaf. And you don't like me. Why? Why?"

"Because," she said. She took his hand and guided it over her blouse, between her open buttons. Then she took his other hand and pressed it between her legs, smooth and cool. De Luca opened his eyes. He caught his breath and closed his fingers around the warm fabric of her shorts, trying to kiss her on the lips, pushing her face against his, but she pulled away with a start. She pushed him back, reached into the opening of his pants and took hold of him, making him groan, then quickly slipped out of her own pants, kicking them off onto the floor. She mounted him, and as he moaned, "Francesca. Oh God, Francesca . . ." she started moving, fast, looking at him all the while, her chin held high and those cold eyes, cold and mean, staring straight into his.

CHAPTER SEVEN

That morning, instead of Leonardi himself, one of his officers came to pick up De Luca. A young, thin boy with a sleepy look about him. He dropped De Luca in front of the town hall. De Luca went in and immediately stopped in the middle of the corridor. He had no idea where to go and stood there until Mayor Savioli came out of a door with his glasses in his hand. He was polishing the lenses with a handkerchief and he only noticed De Luca when he had finished.

"Oh, Engineer! Good morning . . . How are you feeling today?"

"Fine," said De Luca, though it wasn't true at all. "I'm looking for Brigadier Leonardi."

A smile escaped Savioli; a controlled movement that flattened out his lips and closed his eyes ever so slightly. De Luca noticed and felt uneasy.

"Over there," said the Mayor, pointing to a door that had just been opened, and then he shook De Luca's hand, hurriedly. "I don't want to waste your time," he said, lowering his voice, De Luca's hand still in his. "But rest assured I'm on your side. Always have been. And congratulations!"

De Luca nodded, confused, and walked away down the corridor. Savioli was still looking at him. De Luca didn't understand the mayor's words at all, but he was scared and he opened the door to Leonardi's office without knocking. Leonardi looked up from a pile of papers scattered on his desk.

"I just ran into the Mayor who—" began De Luca, but Leonardi interrupted him; harsh.

"Good work, Engineer! Damn good work!"

De Luca frowned. "Sorry?" he said.

"Screwing la Tedeschina, what a fantastic idea. Congratulations! Carnera will be overjoyed! I leave you alone for a second and you create a damn mess: you get drunk, pass out—"

"How do you know?"

"Don't be ridiculous! They were all there at the inn with you!"

"No, I mean about Francesca . . . about la Tedeschina."

"She told me herself, this morning. By now, the whole town knows. What did you think? That she gave herself to you because of your beautiful eyes? She only did it to spite Carnera, to make him jealous."

De Luca held his arms open wide, and then dropped them to his sides. He was shocked. He felt like a fool and he couldn't help himself from laughing.

"Seems like everybody in this town wants to use me for something," he muttered with an embarrassed smile.

"Go ahead! Laugh!" said Leonardi, serious. "Sure, it's a riot . . . I don't know about where you come from, Engineer, but here in our neck of the woods, in Romagna, fooling around with someone else's woman has always been a good way to earn yourself an ounce of lead, and from folks a good deal more civilized than Carnera. How do you think Tedeschina's kraut met his end? He's down a well. Just for the record, they call it the German's Well. I'm doing all I can to save your skin as it is, so avoid drawing attention to yourself, if you don't mind."

De Luca lowered his head, closed his eyes, and clenched his fists. He let out a nervous sigh.

"I'm sorry," he said. "I'm really sorry . . . Okay? What else do you want me to do?"

"I want you to sit down and help me sort out this mess once and for all."

De Luca opened his eyes: "So, we're going ahead?" he asked, incredulous, and the relief made his voice shake.

"Of course! Why wouldn't we? It's my duty to conduct an investigation into what happened and I'm not backing down. What is it, Engineer? Why are you laughing?"

De Luca shook his head, covering his mouth with his hand. He was so relieved he couldn't control himself. He sat down and looked around him, observing the sparsely furnished room—a table, two chairs, a kitchen sideboard stuffed with papers and two faded square patches on the walls, one larger than the other, Mussolini and the King, carted off to who knows where. When he lowered his eyes, they met Leonardi's again, grim, and he quit smiling.

"Let's be honest, Brigadier," said De Luca. "I've been . . . No, I was in the police for far too long not to know how things work. You have just been assured political backing from your Mayor. If that weren't the case, the investigation would never have started in the first place. What did you tell him about me? Does he know who I am?"

Leonardi shook his head. "No," he said. "He thinks you're a party official from Bologna who's here to see how things are going."

"And how *are* things going?"

Leonardi shrugged. "You've seen for yourself: Carnera on one side, Savioli on the other, Bedeschi in the middle acting as mediator. You see, Engineer, Carnera is a legend around here, a hero, one of those heroes with a capital H. He did things during the war . . . Good God! The Black Brigades in Bologna got hold of him and tortured him for two days straight. But nothing doing! Not so much as a word . . . And as if that wasn't enough, the minute they let their guard down, he killed two of them and ran off with their weapons!

He's a legend, Carnera. But over time, he's become an awkward legend, he doesn't want to step aside and Savioli wouldn't mind at all if he came out of this investigation cut down to size a little."

"And you? Would you mind?"

Leonardi frowned and looked to one side.

"Carnera is a partisan and a communist," he said softly. "And I'm a partisan and a communist, too. I hope . . . No, I'm sure things won't come to that."

De Luca sighed. He slid forward in his chair, placing the heels of his shoes on the floor, and put his hands behind his head. The vertebrae in his neck cracked, painfully.

"The way I see it," he said to the ceiling as Leonardi leaned forward, his arms on the desk, "it's self-evident that the Guerras were killed because of that brooch and that they got it from one of those men involved in the action against the count. That is, Pietrino Zauli, this Baroncini fellow, or Carnera. Don't interrupt me, please."

Leonardi had just opened his mouth, but he closed it immediately with a short sigh.

"Apart from the fact," De Luca continued, "that we don't know what the hell this Baroncini has got to do with it, because he wasn't supposed to be there that night, but he was . . . Listen, is it possible to talk with this character? Where is he?"

Leonardi opened his arms. "Not here anymore. Baroncini left town yesterday. He went to Bologna, but nobody knows where exactly."

"Fine, fine . . . apart from all this, then, the first question is why. Why did Delmo Guerra have that brooch? Could it have been payment for something he did? I imagine not, given his situation." Leonardi shook his head, still not saying a word. "So, the question is somewhat different; you can be paid for doing something, but you can also be paid for *not* doing something, for example, not telling people what you know. We engineers call it 'blackmail.'"

Leonardi opened his mouth again, but the only sound that came out was a hoarse wheeze. He stood up, and walked around his desk as he cleared his throat, shaking his head.

"What is it? Something doesn't add up?" De Luca asked.

"Of course it adds up! But in Bologna or Milan, not here! I mean, what on earth would that animal Delmo have had to keep quiet about?"

"For example, when he was off hunting one night, he saw . . ." De Luca stopped, frowned, and Leonardi nodded, unequivocally.

"He did! He saw the count being liquidated. Signor Engineer, nobody wants to talk about it but we all know. Even me, and I'm the police. But I'm not about to arrest Carnera, Pietrino, or Baroncini because they eliminated some son of a bitch spy. Far from it!"

"Okay, but if he had called the carabinieri—"

"The last time we saw two carabinieri around here it was for a town dance. May Day. We disarmed them and sent them home. You see this pistol? It's a gift of the Benemerita.[1] No, Engineer, around here the only ones who get any respect are the Allies, and they're in Bologna. And they only worry about their own problems, thank God. No, it'll be a good while before the carabinieri are able to scare folks like Pietrino and Baroncini!"

"And Carnera."

Leonardi shrugged. "We'll see," he said.

"Fine, we'll see. Listen, here's another motive for blackmail. Guerra knew that someone had pocketed the count's wares and he wanted a cut. They gave him a brooch to keep him happy and then they killed him."

---

[1] "Benemerita": name given to the Carabinieri corps. (Tr.)

"Yes, maybe . . ."

"Ah, finally."

"But not Carnera! I'd swear by it!"

"Oh Christ! Who is this man, a saint?"

Leonardi slammed his fist down on the desk, a sharp blow with his knuckles. "Not a saint, a hero, Engineer, like I told you. Carnera would never, *never*, pocket a single lira belonging to the CLN, nor would he let anybody else." He stopped, and fell silent for a moment; then he turned and with two quick steps went over to De Luca who, surprised, opened his eyes and lifted his head suddenly. His stiff neck cracked.

"I'll tell you a good motive!" Leonardi grabbed him by the sleeve of his trench coat, and shook. "If Carnera had learned that Baroncini or Pietrino or anyone else had stolen something while he was upstairs with the count he would have killed them on the spot. He's done it before! That's what Guerra had to keep quiet about!"

"Yes, yes. It's possible . . . That would make a lot of things add up, like Pietrino's motorcycle being at the Guerras' that night. We've got enough to bring him in . . ."

"Bring him in?" Leonardi stopped rubbing his hands together, impatient, and looked at De Luca, worried. "Bring him in, like, *really bring him in*?"

De Luca got up from the chair and smoothed down his trench coat. "Brigadier, you can't conduct an investigation like this theorizing around a table without so much as an interrogation or a search. And don't forget, that ring is still floating around somewhere and if it happens to show up in Pietrino's house . . ." He wanted to add *It would solve a lot of our problems,* but Leonardi got the idea and nodded, determined.

"Let's go get Pietrino," he said, heading towards the door. "But, good Lord, it's not going to be easy."

Pietrino Zauli wasn't at home. They pulled up in the middle of the barnyard and Leonardi went to knock on the door followed by an officer with a machine gun slung over his shoulder. A woman, barely poking her face out of the door, said something in dialect. All De Luca understood was that Pietrino wasn't there. A second later Leonardi came back to the jeep, in a hurry, and jumped into the driver's seat. He took off suddenly. The thin officer with the sleepy look wasn't even all the way back in the jeep. Leonardi drove fast without saying a word as De Luca clung to the dashboard grip to keep from being thrown out of the jeep every time it hit a pothole. They screeched to a halt in front of a long farmhouse with a low porch and watched as a young boy ran in from the fields and disappeared into a side door. Leonardi punched the steering wheel.

"Son of a bitch!" he growled. "They've already warned him. We did the same thing with the Germans, a young kid and off you go . . . Let's hope he's still here."

They got out of the jeep and only then did the intense, heavy odor hit De Luca in the gut, making him grimace, and draining the blood from his face. A sharp cry came from the farmhouse, followed by others, and still others, even sharper and stronger. De Luca stopped in his tracks. Leonardi noticed and put his hand on De Luca's arm.

"They're pigs, Engineer." He had to yell to make himself heard over the cries. "This is a pig farm and they're slaughtering the pigs. Don't they do this sort of thing where you come from?"

De Luca swallowed and nodded. He followed Leonardi to the door and waited beside him as the young officer went in to look for Pietrino. The noise was so loud it filled his ears and penetrated his brain—awful, piercing cries. When the noise suddenly stopped it almost hurt. A heavy silence fell, as heavy as the odor pressing in on them, and out of the blue De

Luca's nose began to bleed. He held the back of his hand against his nose as a wave of wet warmth descended over his lips, and he staggered. He sat down on a rock, his back against a fencepost, breathing slowly through his mouth.

"What do you want?"

Pietrino Zauli was a small man wearing a black beret pushed forward over his forehead and a red kerchief knotted about his thin, creased neck, baked brown by the sun. One of his eyes was half closed, a pale scar split his eyebrow in half and ran halfway down his cheek, and in his hand, still stained with blood, he was carrying a pruning hatchet with a curved blade. Leonardi swallowed, wetting his lips with his tongue.

"I have to ask you some things, Pietrino," he said. "Some important things."

"I'm busy right now. Come back later."

"Were you at Guerra's house the night he died?"

"Why?"

"Your motorbike was in Delmo's courtyard that day. What were you doing there?"

"Why?

Leonardi clenched his fists and closed his eyes for a second, just one second.

"Pietrino," he hissed, "if you don't give me an answer here, I'll arrest you and you'll give it to me down at the station."

"Yeah? Who do you think you are, Guido, a carabiniere?"

Pietrino Zauli took a step forward and Leonardi took one back. Pietrino pointed the pruning hatchet at De Luca as if it were a sword. "And who's this? He a carabiniere, too?"

De Luca made a face as the bittersweet taste of blood spread over his top lip. He tilted his head back, and sniffled. Behind a window, half-sitting on the windowsill, there was a man with a rifle across his knees. Leonardi noticed him too. He closed his eyes again, this time for two seconds.

"You're coming with me. We can do it the easy way, or the hard way. What do you say, Pietrino?"

Pietrino shook his head, rubbing his tortoise neck against the red kerchief.

"Not the hard way, and not the easy way, Guido. What do you think you're doing? What're you sticking your nose into? You know what they say around here . . . If you see something black, shoot: either it's a priest or a carabiniere. I see black, Guido, a whole lot of black. Be careful."

"Watch out, Pietrino . . . Don't pull too hard on the rope!"

Leonardi moved his hand, not in the direction of his holster but lifting it ever so slightly, tightening the muscles of his wrist. Pietrino pushed his beret back using the same hand that was holding the pruning knife and then put his hands on his hips.

"Go ahead, then . . ." he said. "Go ahead and play cop. I'll be here doing a man's work . . . along with everything else. You wanna know where I was that day? I was with Lea all day. Now go take one up the ass, you and your buddy here." He turned and slowly walked back to the door. Leonardi muttered weakly, "Stop, Pietrino!" But Pietrino didn't stop.

"Three times with Lea . . ." he said without turning, straightening his arm, his fingers extended. "Three times!" he repeated before disappearing. The door closed with a sharp bang. Inside, the pigs began squealing again and De Luca tilted his head back, groaning. Leonardi turned and walked off in the direction of the jeep. The officer with the sleepy look had left his machine gun lying on the seat and wandered off some time ago, heading across the fields with his hands in his pockets.

CHAPTER EIGHT

"**A** nosebleed . . . Like a little kid! Are you sure you used to be a policeman?" Leonardi's tone was bitter. His voice was high-pitched and hoarse.

De Luca held his neck straight, trying to soften the blows of the jeep. He had tried leaning his head back against the headrest, but every pothole in the road sent a jarring blow right through him.

"If you want to blame me, go right ahead . . . There's nothing I can do about it."

"Right, I see that you're an expert at doing nothing. A nosebleed! Didn't you ever hear them scream like stuck pigs back when you were with your friends?"

"Who is this Lea?"

"Who? Oh, Lea . . . Pietrino's woman, she works at the cooperative. Why?"

"Because Pietrino said he was with her that day and he strikes me as being the type of man who's too sure of himself to think he might need an alibi. If we get to her before they warn her, maybe we could catch them with conflicting stories. That is, if he is our—"

De Luca didn't even manage to finish his sentence. Leonardi pushed the accelerator down right in the middle of a pothole and the jeep leaped forward, suddenly, one side lifting off the ground, and almost ended up in a ditch.

"How should I put it to her?" Leonardi already had one

leg out of the jeep when he stopped to cough, embarrassed, into his closed fist. "If I say, 'Was Pietrino with you the day they killed Guerra?' she'll catch on and she'll say, 'Of course he was. Of course. So?'"

De Luca put his hand on his chin, reflecting, and then shrugged.

"Tell her you didn't know that she and Pietrino had split up."

"What do you mean, split up?"

"Right, that's more or less what Lea will say. Then tell her you saw Pietrino that day with another woman and watch her reaction. Either she says it's impossible because he was with her, or she goes berserk and Pietrino lied to us. And maybe he's our man."

"Right!" Leonardi slapped him on the shoulder with the back of his hand and got out of the jeep. De Luca remained sitting in the jeep, pulling his trench coat tight, shaken by a cold chill. It was a strange morning, the sun came and went, and though there were no storm clouds in the sky it seemed as if it was going to rain at any moment. Pietrino Zauli . . . De Luca said the name over again, under his voice, moving his lips slightly, then shook his head. Maybe, he thought. Maybe . . .

Something touched him on the arm, making him jump, and he hit his knee against the dashboard.

"Oh God, I'm sorry! I scared you."

Veniero Bedeschi pulled his hand back as if it had been burned, then smiled, his white-haired moustache straight as a line on his upper lip.

"How are you today, Engineer?" he said. "You seem paler than ever. Come with me and I'll treat you to a glass of wine . . . Ah, perhaps not, given that it doesn't agree with you. Well, let's go to the barber's; he makes a little coffee-flavored liquor that brings the dead back to life. Right here, across the street, no excuses now . . ."

He held out his hand towards De Luca, who shook his head, touching his stomach as he did so. But Bedeschi already had him by the arm and was pulling him out. He slipped down from the jeep, catching his trench coat on the mudguard.

"I'm waiting for Brigadier Leonardi," he said, pointing at the door to the cooperative with his thumb. "Waiting on some documents, urgent docu—"

"Don't worry, Engineer, we'll see your brigadier from the door. Come on."

De Luca let himself be taken underarm, docilely. The idea of the coffee-flavored liquor made his empty stomach growl painfully and drew him almost violently across the street. He had to stop himself from pushing Bedeschi along. They entered the barbershop, a long, narrow room, with a mirror on the wall and three wooden chairs in front of it. There was a short little man in a white tunic leaning on a basin. He was parting his hair, a precise part right above his ear, and combing long strands of hair over the bald crown of his head.

"Please, have a seat, Engineer. And now that you're here, why don't you get yourself a shave? Marino is first-class, you know?"

De Luca ran his hand over his cheek, instinctively, and shaking his head said, "No, thank you." He did need a shave, his beard was prickling his neck and had been bothering him for several days, but the promise of that liquor made him feel as if he might faint. He wouldn't have swapped it for anything, not even for a tub full of lavender bath salts. Bedeschi seemed to read his mind.

"Marino, give us a bit of that stuff of yours, will you? The Engineer here needs a little pick-me-up."

De Luca smiled. He sat down and put his hands in the pockets of his trench coat. He looked up at his reflection in the mirror, but then immediately lowered his eyes again. He really did seem like a hobo; he even had a speck of congealed blood on his lip, which he scratched away without anyone seeing. Bedeschi, on the other hand, looked at his reflection openly and with obvious satisfaction, slicking back his gray hair.

"Time goes by for all of us, Engineer," he said. "Though perhaps it's gone by faster for us. Me, for example, how old do you think I am? Go on, tell me . . ."

De Luca shrugged, screwing up his face. "Fifty?" he said, thinking principally of all that gray hair.

"Forty-two. But it's as though you hit the nail on the head, because I spent a year in Germany, which counts for ten years. And you, I reckon you'd be about thirty-five, thirty-six . . . Am I right?"

"Give or take . . ." said De Luca.

"But the past doesn't matter. What counts is the future. Are you more interested in the past or the future, Engineer?"

De Luca raised his eyes and realized that Bedeschi was watching him in the mirror, a keen look in his eyes and, beneath the white strip of moustache, that straight smile on his lips.

"Depends," said De Luca.

"On what?"

"Depends on the future."

Marino came in from out back, passing through a faded rattan curtain that made a hollow, knocking sound as it closed in his wake. He was carrying three glasses in his hand and a black corked bottle under his arm. De Luca licked his lips.

"Now, I'm going to tell you a story, Engineer," said Bedeschi, taking the bottle from Marino and pouring two fingers of liquor in a glass. "In '44 I got caught in a big dragnet operation and they sent me to a concentration camp. Never been so hungry in my life! There wasn't a thing to eat, nothing! I weighed forty-five kilos when the Indians liberated us, and they gave us rice cooked in a chamber pot. I swear! But you want a laugh, Engineer? Every so often I get my wife to cook me rice that way, in a bedpan. It takes me back, back to the taste of that rice . . . And do you know the point of all this? That we need to forget the past's ugly moments, and hang on to the good ones."

A smile escaped De Luca's lips.

"If only it were possible." He reached and took the glass Bedeschi was holding out to him.

"It is, Engineer. It is . . . You only have to look to the future. Take our Marino, for example. He was just a floor boy in this shop. The barber was another fellow, a suspicious type, who was always running around with members of the Black Brigades. One day, two strangers showed up and shot him, the barber, just as Marino was closing up shop."

Marino nodded earnestly and a thin strand of hair fell over his forehead.

"One of them leaned his pistol on my shoulder, and fired . . . two shots, *bang bang!*"

"Exactly. Our Marino here went deaf in one ear for three days and his legs were trembling for a week, but it all passed. Now he's ordering new chairs for the shop, and in the meantime he concocts this liquor, which is a genuine wonder. What do you think, Engineer? Isn't this stuff here better than the horrible details of an isolated moment that is best forgotten?"

"Why are you telling me all this?" said De Luca, hoarse. While Bedeschi was talking he had drunk a mouthful of liquor and the bitter taste of coffee thickened his tongue. The alcohol, on the other hand, made him feel lighter and more alert. He felt as if his eyes were wide open. He had to look at himself in the mirror to be sure.

"Because the future means reconstruction, and that's a matter for engineers like you. There are big plans for Sant'Alberto, you know? Companies born from nothing that now look exceptionally promising, Engineer. There's Baroncini, for example."

"Baroncini?" De Luca turned his eyes to Bedeschi, who was staring at something in his glass, intently.

"Right, Baroncini. He bought himself two trucks from the English and set up a transportation company that'll mean jobs for half the town."

"He must have been awfully rich, this Baroncini. Two trucks don't come cheap."

"No, he wasn't rich . . . but he's a clever sort of fellow and he found the money. There you have it, Engineer: Baroncini poor is the past; Baroncini with a business that'll create wealth for lots of people is the future."

"And Baroncini who stumbles upon the investment capital belongs to the past."

Bedeschi smiled, lifting his eyes up from the glass.

"Bravo, Engineer! Why it's clear as anything that you have been to university. Look! The Brigadier is coming out of the cooperative as we speak . . ."

De Luca went to stand up but Marino held him down, pulling a comb out of a pocket in his tunic with a flourish.

"Stop right there, Engineer. You may let your beard grow as you wish, though it doesn't become you. But no man has ever left my shop with hair in such a state!"

Leonardi was standing on the jeep's running board, holding onto the seat, and looking around, worried. De Luca waved, his arm held high, and walked hurriedly towards him, almost running. He felt euphoric.

"I was at the barber's," he said, breathing a little heavy. "He insisted on spraying me with this smelly stuff . . . What's the matter?"

Leonardi's face was dark, troubled. There was a woman

beside him. She wasn't tall, her body was heavy, solid, and wide cheekbones protruded from her flat face.

"Tell him what you told me, Lea," said Leonardi, touching her on the shoulder.

"Pietrino didn't get it up three times. He fell asleep like a log after the first."

"Come on, Lea. Good god!" Leonardi touched her again, giving her a shove. "Tell him the way you told me, and seriously! He's the Engineer."

The woman shrugged and nodded, as if there were no need to add anything. She reached under her floral print dress with her fingers and adjusted the shoulder strap of her petticoat.

"Pietrino was with me that day, so it's impossible that somebody saw him with another woman. And lucky for him! Otherwise I'd have ripped out the one good eye he's got. And anyway, who'd want someone like Pietrino, ugly as he is? Only me . . ."

"How long were you with him?" De Luca put his elbow on the mudguard of the jeep and leaned forward, staring at the woman. She took a step back.

"Who's the Brigadier here, you or him?" she said.

"How long was Pietrino Zauli with you?" he said.

"Long time . . . He came over and picked me up and we went to the river, to a place he knows, a hunting cabin. It must have taken us half an hour to get there."

"On motorbike it takes ten minutes," said Leonardi. "But . . ."

"But he wasn't on his bike, like I told you . . . He took me there by bicycle, perched on the handlebars. And it mightn't look it, but I weigh—"

De Luca held his hand up, interrupting her.

"How long were you there, at the river?"

"All afternoon. Then Pietrino fell asleep and we went to

the villa, to eat, and on the way back he was drunk and we fell into a ditch. It's all my brother's fault."

"Your brother?"

"Yeah, Gianni." The woman fixed the other shoulder strap, adjusting her dress. "He doesn't want me to see Pietrino, because of that story with the black market. Pietrino isn't afraid of anyone, it's just that—"

"Pietrino Zauli plays on the black market?" asked De Luca, astounded. Leonardi shook his head and raised his voice to shut the woman up as she was about to continue.

"No, Engineer. He's not the type. It's just that one night he borrowed Gianni's van, a coal-burning Fiat 1100, and didn't bring it back until the next day."

"All right, but what's the black market got to do with us?"

The woman was quicker this time. "It's not that Pietrino borrowed the van . . . Carnera came and got it the night before, Pietrino just brought it back, all dirty with blood. But Gianni wasn't angry about that. When he has to, he carries slaughtered animals too. But Pietrino was rude, as usual, and so Gianni—"

De Luca straightened up and nodded, distracted. He got into the jeep on the driver's side and raised his legs over the gear stick to slide over to the other side. Leonardi said goodbye to the woman and got in too.

"This blows everything," he said, grim.

De Luca started.

"How's that?"

"Pietrino has an alibi, one we can check. He didn't kill the Guerras."

"Of course not! It's obvious. But that's not what I was thinking about. No, I was thinking something else. The van . . . it wasn't used to transport animals, was it? I'll bet it was the night of May seventh . . ."

Leonardi sighed deeply. "The night of the count, yes . . . But so what? That's been cleared up, right?"

"Yes, but there's something odd about it . . . Why didn't Carnera load the count into the car? It would have been easier. Sure, it can get crowded in a Topolino, but did he really have to come all this way to borrow a van? And then, this story about Pietrino's motorcycle . . . This red motorbike riding around all of Romagna with nobody on it annoys me . . . Why didn't he have it the other night? Why was he on a bicycle? Who did he lend it to? Does he usually lend it to someone in particular?"

Leonardi clenched the steering wheel, tense. "You'd have to ask him. But then blood starts streamin' out of your nose."

"Drop it, Brigadier. But let's think about this Baroncini fellow. All of a sudden he gets rich and buys himself two trucks."

Leonardi turned to him, surprised. "And how do you know about that?"

"I'm an engineer, remember? You, on the other hand, you knew about it and it didn't occur to you . . . When did he buy these trucks? And how did he pay for them? In cash, or some other way? A ring, perhaps? Get in touch with the English and find out."

Leonardi smiled, shaking his head. "At your command, Engineer. And you? Where shall I take you?"

De Luca nodded, decidedly. "Home, please. That is, to the inn. I'm feeling hungry, finally."

Chapter Nine

When he got out of the jeep in front of the inn, De Luca was reminded of the mayor, and Carnera, and all people who'd be there at that hour, and as he was making his way around the house to go in through the back door a thin boy wearing a striped tank top ran into him, banging against his knee. The boy took two steps back, staggering, then looked at him, afraid, and quickly bent his bony elbow, bringing his hand up to his forehead in a salute. De Luca smiled, surprised, massaging his knee, and he didn't have time to say a word before the boy shot off. He went around the corner of the house then stopped suddenly, frozen by a hoarse, muffled cry. La Tedeschina was in the middle of the yard holding a writhing chicken in the air by its feet, its wings flapping in its final spasms of life. She lifted her eyes and looked at him, hard, as usual.

"What's the matter? Does this bother you?"

De Luca shook his head, but the fact was that yes, it did bother him a little. There was a chair in the middle of the yard. La Tedeschina sat down, placed the chicken in her lap and started plucking its feathers from the tail up.

"Sometimes it's less upsetting to see a man killed than a chicken," said De Luca. La Tedeschina shrugged, her face indifferent.

"I seen chickens dead and men dead and neither of 'em bothers me," she said. De Luca nodded. He watched her for a while longer as she plucked away with quick flicks of her wrist, then he picked up an empty fruit crate, turned it on its end, and sat down next to her, balanced on the crate. Another chicken came over and clucked suspiciously, giving him a sidelong glance.

"I don't like the country," said De Luca. "When I was little my parents took me out to the country every Sunday and I never knew what to do. I'd chase the chickens but then they'd yell at me because I'd get sweaty. The smoke from the fire gave me a headache and I just couldn't figure out how to walk across that cloddy ploughed earth."

La Tedeschina shook her hand to remove the feathers that were stuck to her fingers.

"It's plain to see you're a city type," she said. De Luca was surprised as he thought she wasn't listening. "Though from the looks of it, I'd say you're more like a gypsy."

"I must still look a little distinguished, though. Just now a little boy saluted me like I was an army officer."

La Tedeschina looked at him and smiled, a cunning smile, full of meaning.

"I know who you are," she said. De Luca started, making the crate creak.

"Who am I?" he said. La Tedeschina nodded.

"I know. Everybody knows." She glanced at him, her black eyes flashing. "You're a carabiniere."

De Luca opened his mouth but all that came out was a whimper, half way between surprise and relief.

"Me? What a thought! No, I'm not a carabiniere. Really. I'm . . . I'm an engineer. Seriously . . ."

La Tedeschina nodded again, the same sly smile on her lips, then she moved, leaned back in the chair and stretched her legs out over his knees. De Luca gulped, stiff, uneasy. Once more that heavy sensation, soft and damp, pressing on his insides, almost hurting him. He felt the warmth of her skin through the fabric of his pants. He realized his hands were shaking.

"Anyway, it's not important who I am," he said, hoarsely. "I don't even know myself." He raised his hand, hesitant, and with his finger he touched the pale scrape on her knee. She let him do it, then suddenly said: "Don't touch me!" She shifted her legs brusquely. De Luca turned a violent red and pulled his hand away.

"I don't like carabinieri," she said coldly. "And you're too thin. And you ain't got no marks. Carnera says you can't be a real man if you don't have marks from the war."

De Luca threw his arms open wide. "Yeah, well, it's clear that I'm not a real man. I bet Carnera is full of marks."

"Yeah. Lots."

"Great. Good man . . . But then, I didn't go to war. At least, not to the front, as a soldier . . . Ow!"

La Tedeschina had taken her legs off him so quickly she hit his knee with the heel of her clog, which had come off her foot and bounced into his hand. She jumped to her feet and started searching the pockets of her tunic.

"Pietrino's motorbike!" she said.

"Motorbike?" De Luca asked. Then he too noticed the intermittent throb of a motorbike coming from the other side of the house. La Tedeschina pulled a dark hanky from her pocket.

"Yeah, a motorbike! It belongs to Pietrino but it's usually Carnera who's on it. If he sees me like this, he'll kill me . . . He was the one who cut my hair and now he wants me to wear a handkerchief!" She folded it into a triangle and laid it over her forehead, but then snatched it off again and stuck it in her pocket.

"But I'm not gonna!" she said, lifting her chin up. She sat back down and put the chicken back on her knee, violently plucking the last few feathers from its corpse. De Luca hadn't moved. He was lost in thought, only partly aware of what was happening, preoccupied with a vague thought that had just flashed through his mind and vanished with that sharp blow to the knee. The keen fear that had left him breathless confounded his thoughts even more when he saw Carnera coming across the yard, determined, heading straight for them.

"Put the headscarf on!" roared Carnera. La Tedeschina lowered her eyes even more, bending towards the chicken, searching its yellow flesh with her fingers for one last nonexistent feather. Carnera clenched his jaw and De Luca saw the tendons in his neck tighten beneath his dark skin.

"Put your headscarf on now!" he said again. "You look ridiculous with that hair!"

"Some reckon I'm beautiful just like I am!" said la Tedeschina, lifting her eyes. She was about to stick her tongue out but Carnera grabbed her by the cheek with his enormous hand. He lifted her out of her chair and shook her violently as she hung from his arm and attempted to kick him. She finally managed to break free, dropping to his side and slipping away. She ran straight into the house.

De Luca hadn't moved. He hadn't even gotten up from his crate. Sitting there, her shoe in his hand, like a fool. Carnera breathed heavily, his fists clenched, then turned towards him.

"I'm not crazy, Engineer," he said. "Savioli and his gang would pay millions to see me fuck up, but I know that this isn't the time or the place to go killing a carabiniere. That's the only reason you're still alive, Engineer." He stretched out the "eer" and leered threateningly. De Luca stood up, but Carnera put a hand on his shoulder, forcing him to sit back down on the crate.

"What are you thinking, you and that fool, Guido? What do you think you represent here? The law? Whose law? I make the law here, and I know better than you what justice means. Tell Guido what I told you, that is, if he's interested in saving his skin. As for you, Engineer, there's no hope. You won't be leaving Sant'Alberto. You're already dead."

De Luca swallowed, with difficulty, as he tilted his head back to look up. Carnera pointed a finger at his forehead.

"You have been informed," he said through his clenched teeth. "You have been informed."

Francesca was alone in the kitchen. She was quartering the chicken and the minute she saw him she brought the knife down hard onto the cutting board, neatly severing the chicken's featherless neck.

"You're a coward," she said, hard.

De Luca sat down near the fire, his elbows on his knees and his face in his hands. The smell of meat and blood turned his stomach.

"No," he said. "I'm not a coward, but I'm afraid. I'm afraid like a hunted animal. There's a difference."

"You disgust me! You're a coward and you disgust me!"

De Luca sighed. "All right, okay, I'm a coward. But right now I have to find a way to save my skin and maybe . . . maybe there's a way. Earlier, you said—"

"I'm not saying another word!" The knife came down again onto the cutting board with a sharp whack that made De Luca jump and close his eyes.

"Listen, Francesca," he said softly. "Call me whatever you want—coward, bastard, fascist, faggot—but I've got this one idea in my head now and I'm only interested in that. You said Carnera is a real man because he's got the marks of war all over him. Where are these marks?"

La Tedeschina frowned. The absurdity of his question calmed her and for a moment she just stood there staring at him with the knife in her hand, leaning on the table, her bare foot held against her knee.

"Why?"

"Where are they?"

"He's got a lot . . . On his shoulder, on his back . . . And scars on his stomach, straight across his stomach, from when the fascists got him in Bologna. But why—"

"Another thing . . . When you were putting the kerchief over your head—who knows via what association, but apparently fear makes me think better—I thought of something. Do you remember that night when we . . . when you told me that you didn't belong to anyone—"

"I don't belong to anyone," she repeated, hard, and De Luca quickly picked up his question, nodding, before she started insulting him again.

"Yes, yes, I know. But that night you told me Carnera had given you a gift. What did he give you?" De Luca stood up and she took a step back and leaned against the sink. For the first time, she looked unsure of herself.

"Why do you want to know?" she said. "You're scaring me . . . I'm not telling."

De Luca smiled. "Carnera didn't give you anything. It was a lie. Carnera doesn't give gifts."

"Yes he did!"

"Maybe a flower . . ."

"It wasn't a flower! He gave me a ring, a blue ring, big as anything . . . And I threw it into the river!"

De Luca closed his eyes and sighed deeply, emptying his lungs of air and freeing his clenched stomach of the nausea that had come over him when he entered.

"I knew it," he said. "Thanks, Francesca."

He turned and left the kitchen. When he reached the door she started screaming again, "Coward!" But he didn't notice. He was buried in thought. He didn't even notice the clog that was still in the pocket of his trench coat.

CHAPTER TEN

"It was Carnera. We both knew it from the start, only we did everything we could to sidestep the fact. But it was him."

On his feet, in the middle of the police station, De Luca was virtually shaking with excitement. Leonardi, on the other hand, was staring at him, serious, with one eyebrow raised and his forearms on his desk, attentive and alert, like at school. De Luca waited for a comment that didn't come.

"So, listen," he said, sticking his thumb up and waving it in the air. "First: the motorbike. Carnera uses it often, so it could have been him at the Guerra's house that night and not Pietrino. But you knew this, even though you didn't tell me. Second." His index finger went up next to his thumb, midair, like an open V. "When Carnera was taken by the fascist brigade in Bologna he learned at his own expense a very special way of interrogating. And he tortured Delmo in that exact same way, just like the fascists."

"Easy, Engineer! There's quite a difference between Carnera and the fascists!"

De Luca nodded. "Yes, yes, of course . . . I meant their methods. Anyway . . . Third: the jewelry. Carnera found jewelry in the count's house, the brooch, and a sapphire ring, which he pocketed . . . I know, I know what you're thinking." Leonardi was shaking his head and De Luca came closer, his arms held out before him, "Carnera wouldn't have kept anything for himself, he's a hero and he lives like a Spartan. But good Lord, Leonardi, even heroes have hearts! He pocketed them to give to la Tedeschina, a flashy gift, to shake her up a little! You must agree the girl is capable of making a man lose his head with that way of hers . . ."

Leonardi continued shaking his head, his hands held up like he was about to slap them over his ears.

"This only explains why he had the ring, Engineer, but nothing else! I know where you're going with this; I've just figured it out for myself. Guerra found out about the jewelry and Carnera gave him the brooch to keep him quiet until he could find a way to kill him. But that doesn't make any sense . . ."

De Luca frowned, irritated, and crossed his arms over his chest.

"You keep forgetting who Carnera is," said Leonardi. "If he wanted, he could have the count's entire house for himself and nobody would say anything. At most he'd lose a little respect. It's not enough for blackmail, not with Carnera. It's not motive enough, Engineer."

"Don't you think it's finally time to ask him directly?"

"That is?"

"Arrest him. Learco Padovani, known as Carnera, is the prime suspect in this case and therefore we ought to arrest him and question him."

Leonardi stood up, sending his chair sliding across the floor. He went over to the window and looked out, as if the conversation no longer interested him.

"And how?" he said, distracted.

"Using correct police procedure, not backwoods ones. Give me four men and I'll take care of it. You have political backing, the mayor's blessing . . . You should be able to find four men, right?"

Leonardi breathed onto the glass pane and drew a line with his finger, staring at it until it disappeared, quickly.

"Savioli was here a while back," he said and his words took De Luca's breath away. "It sounded like Bedeschi talking . . . *We're all comrades, all brothers, let sleeping dogs lie* . . . I finally got him to tell me what happened. This morning he was walking in front of the mill; somebody fired two shots into the wall. He felt them go by, right in front of his face."

"All right, all right . . ." De Luca's voice was shaking and he rubbed his lips with his hand. "But maybe we can do it anyway. Maybe, if we tried—"

"I'm not going to arrest Carnera on my own, Engineer. I can't, and I don't even know if I want to."

"All right . . ." De Luca clenched his fists and closed his eyes, trying to concentrate, standing stock-still in the middle of the room like somebody had planted him there. "I can understand that the count, a fascist spy, doesn't mean anything to you, and that's okay . . . And Guerra, too, a poacher and a thief, okay . . . But the others? Brigadier, the other three?"

Leonardi raised his fist and slammed it hard and fast against the window jamb, making the glass vibrate. "Don't talk shit, Engineer. Please!" he hissed. "The first time the Allies bombed Sant'Alberto it was Monday, market day. There were so many dead bodies that we buried them in wardrobes because there weren't enough coffins. What do you say to that? Should we put the Allies on trial too? Don't talk to me about innocent victims, Engineer: you're not interested in justice, you just want to save your skin. Carnera is going to kill you and that's the only reason you want to arrest him."

"Yes, no . . . I don't know." De Luca clenched his teeth so tight he heard them grinding. Then he moved, finally, and with his arm held out straight, cleared the desk of everything that was on it.

"Good God, Brigadier!" he roared, as Leonardi turned with a start. "We've solved the case, we've got the killer. It's over! Do you want to turn your back on the whole thing just like that? You can't, you can't do that! You're a policeman!"

"Engineer . . ."

"That's enough of this Engineer business!" De Luca cried, so loudly that his words were distorted, echoing in the room. "I am not an Engineer! I am a Police Commissario!" He stood there for a few seconds with his mouth open, panting for breath, then closed it. He swallowed, shutting his eyes and ran his hand over his face, sighing. "I was a Police Commissario," he murmured softly.

Leonardi looked out of the window and gestured angrily at a woman who had stopped to look in the window. He went over to his desk and sat down. He opened a drawer, pushing himself back on the chair's hind legs to reach into the back of the drawer, and rummaged around beneath a pile of papers.

"I don't give a damn who you are, Signor Morandi," he said. "Morandi Giovanni." He threw the ID card at De Luca. It hit him in the stomach and fell to the floor, open.

"Take your papers, sir, and get out of here. Go wherever the hell you want."

CHAPTER ELEVEN

He was looking at the leaves on the most distant tree, waiting for them to grow dark. His forehead, leaned up against the cold glass of the window, was starting to hurt and with every breath the circle of condensation on the window spread to eye-level, veiling the view of the inn's courtyard and unveiling it again, in quick succession, like the fade-ins and fade-outs in dreams, or American movies. At first, he thought he'd better leave immediately, while there was still a little light left, so he wouldn't lose his way. But then he decided it was better to wait, an hour, at least so that he would blend into the gray shadows of nightfall; then another hour, so that it would be darker, then another, because at night . . . The final leaf vanished into a patch of darkness, indistinct, and De Luca bit his lip, sighing, fogging up the window completely. Maybe, he thought, I'd better wait until tomorrow. The first light of dawn . . .

"Engineer!"

La Tedeschina threw open the door behind him, making him jump. De Luca hit his head against the glass, a sharp blow.

"Engineer, what are you doing still here? Come with me!"

She crossed the room, quickly, and grabbed the cuff of his trench coat, almost pulling it off his shoulders.

"Come with me, now! Carnera's on his way here! He's going to kill you!"

De Luca stiffened and his trench coat, taut, made a snapping sound across his back. Then fear loosened his legs and he followed la Tedeschina, who dragged him stumbling, leaning forward, walking fast so as not to fall, from the room.

They went down the stairs and into the backyard. De Luca was heading around the corner of the house but la Tedeschina pulled him in the opposite direction like he was a horse.

"Not that way! You'll run right into him! Over here!"

She slipped out of her shoes and held them in her hands. She ran towards the fields, her elbows held tight against her sides, swift and sure of herself in the dark, stopping only to say, "C'mon, Engineer!" every time De Luca, who could only make out the faint gleam of her bare legs, tripped on the clumps of earth and fell with a dull thud. They entered a barren thicket; only the thorny outlines of the thicket and the straight silhouette of a single tree were visible. La Tedeschina turned and shoved her shoes against De Luca's chest to stop him.

"Okay," she said. "This is it."

There was a hulking shadow around the tree, covered by a tangled mass of branches. His eyes began to adjust to the darkness and through the brambles he made out a straight wall made of wood and a crossbeam running through a steel hoop.

"It's a hunting blind," said la Tedeschina. "But the partisans used it as a hideout. Inside! Go on."

De Luca slid the crossbeam out and pushed the wall open. He had to bend down to get in because the roof was very low. La Tedeschina pushed him to one side and entered too. She moved an empty crate aside and lifted a burlap sack covered in leaves off the ground. Underneath there was a long dark hole.

"There," she said.

De Luca shuddered. "Me? In there?"

"Yes, you! The blind's not the hideout. It's there. The blind's the first place they'll look."

She pushed him so hard De Luca almost fell, slipping on two of the wooden hen-house steps that led into the hole. La Tedeschina picked up the burlap sack and went to cover him but he stopped her, raising his hand and grabbing her by the ankle, which was scratched and cut.

"Francesca," he said, "thank you." She freed herself, jerking away from his hold.

"I don't care a thing about you," she said, hard. "I'm only doing this to make Carnera mad."

De Luca closed his eyes tight and covered his face with his hands as a load of damp dust fell from the sack, getting in his mouth, and making him cough and spit, disgusted. He reopened his eyes to total darkness and caught his breath. Not even the pale light of the moon made it through the crate covering the hole. He reached out gingerly and tapped the solid earth surrounding him, then bent his knees and sat down, straight-backed, without leaning up against anything, hugging his legs. He turned up the collar of his trench coat and shuddered; it was cold and for a moment he envisioned the horrid sight of the disgusting insect he had crushed the moment he entered, and he leaned his forehead against his knees, covering the back of his head with his hands.

Holy Christ, he thought, a nightmare: buried alive in a dark hole cloaked in a silence as cold as a morgue.

The only sound was his own breathing, heavy, slow, and the dull beating of his heart, like veiled thunder booming in his ears, covered by his forearms.

The rustle of fabric against his skin at every slight contraction of his tense muscles.

The rasping groan of his empty stomach.

Then a crash, sudden, deadened by the crate above him and another, louder, followed by a buzzing sound, like a whisper, a murmur, that made his heart beat faster. De Luca closed his eyes even tighter and pushed his wrists against his ears so hard that he heard the blood in his veins pulsing—only the blood, only the blood—until the whispers became voices and steps, determined, in the blind above him and a final crash carried the crate covering his hideaway away with it. The dust from the burlap sack fell down the collar of his shirt.

"Here he is!" somebody said as they grabbed him by the shoulders and pulled him out, his eyes still closed tight. He opened them only when he was thrown against the trunk of the tree and he had to grab at the bark to stop from falling, wrapped in his trench coat.

"Well look who we've got here," said Carnera, pointing the light of an electric torch in his face. "Were you hunting truffles, Engineer?"

De Luca blinked, blinded by the light. He shielded his eyes with one hand and made out two armed men, Carnera, and at his side, holding a gasoline lantern, Pietrino Zauli.

"You can consider yourself the only man who has ever duped Learco Padovani," said Carnera. "But you won't be around to tell the story. Did you read today's paper, Engineer?"

Carnera took a step forward, thrusting an open newspaper in De Luca's face and shining the torch on the page, which turned glossy beneath the light. De Luca squinted and read: "Sentencing Imminent for Rassetto the Butcher." And underneath, blurred and distorted by the light, a photograph. In the far corner, emerging out of the blinding torchlight, cut in half by a fold in the newspaper, with his hands in his pockets, wearing a black shirt under his trench coat, was De Luca.

"To think Savioli was convinced you were a party bigwig," Carnera laughed. "And me, a carabiniere of all things . . . If I think that Francesca . . ." He closed his mouth and, with a straight, sharp movement that cut the air with a whistling sound, hit De Luca on the forehead and sent him to the ground.

"Come on," he said. "Let's get him out of here and do what we have to do."

CHAPTER TWELVE

H e was roused by a pungent odor, a sour disgusting odor that made his stomach tighten and twist. He tried to open his eyes, but could only manage one. He was only able to open the other halfway, as the corner of his eyelid was stuck to his cheek. It came unstuck all of a sudden, painfully tearing the veil from his eyes.

"It was a drunk, the other day . . . He vomited in the corner and I still have to clean it up. But you'll have to make do; it's the only cell we got."

Leonardi was sitting on a stool, outside the room, in the corridor. De Luca, on the other hand, was on the ground, leaning against the wall, his mouth open.

"What . . . am I doing here?" he asked.

"Is that any kind of question for a policeman to be asking? What do people usually do in a cell? You're in jail, you're under arrest."

De Luca cleared his throat. The smell was unbearable and it was filling his mouth with saliva as if he, too, were about to vomit.

"I mean what am I doing here *alive*."

"Right, alive. I saw the paper last night, and I went over to the inn. La Tedeschina told me what happened and where you were and I got there just as they were hauling you off. So I arrested you and took you into custody."

"And Carnera didn't say anything?"

"He said I was getting myself into trouble, but I had this

with me and it shut him up." Leonardi put his hand into his pocket and pulled out a hand grenade, black, small and round. "But it won't last long. I may be wearing a smile, Engineer, but I'm shitting myself."

De Luca raised his arm and reached his hand out to Leonardi, who looked at him, perplexed.

"Come on, Brigadier, help me up, I want out of here."

"Frankly, Engineer, I . . ."

De Luca sighed. "Brigadier, you didn't come to get me because of my monologues about justice . . . You realized we are both in the same boat and that the only way to save our skin is to get the better of Carnera. I know that too, so relax, I'm not going to escape . . . We've already seen that it's no use trying."

Leonardi nodded, held out his arm, and helped De Luca away from the wall with a firm yank.

In the police office at the end of the corridor, De Luca inhaled through his nose until his head started spinning.

"You're covered with blood," said Leonardi. "Do you want a little water?"

De Luca gingerly touched his forehead and grimaced, running his fingertips over the hard scab of a wound.

"We'll take care of it later," he said. "Right now we have more important things to do." He walked around the desk and sat down in Leonardi's chair, engrossed in thought, staring at the ceiling, and biting the inside of his lip. Leonardi, irritated, shot a look at the other chair and sighed.

"The damned season," he said.

De Luca raised his eyes. "What's that?"

"There was a column in *L'Unità* last week that called the summer of '44 'the damned season,' because we were still fighting, still risking our lives . . . The summer of '45 is over too and I'm still fighting."

De Luca shrugged and grinned wearily. "I don't remember

a single summer that wasn't damned. And there are more to come."

Leonardi frowned and shook his head. He noticed a newspaper lying on the sideboard open to the page with De Luca's photograph and smiled, bitter.

"Sure is funny, though," he said. "Here I am, a partisan and a communist, plotting the best way to lock up a comrade. With a fascist."

De Luca stopped staring at the ceiling. He leaned his forearms on the desk, hunched, his head down between his shoulders.

"That's enough of this fascist business," he said.

"Oh yeah? Are you a partisan, too, Engineer?"

"No. I'm a police officer. I was a police officer." De Luca scratched the scab on his forehead, slowly pulling it away with his fingernails. He sighed. "I had been at university for two years when I took an entrance exam for the police academy and was accepted. My parents didn't know, they wanted me to be a lawyer, but I was always reading Gaboriau, Poe's tales, *Murders in the Rue Morgue* . . . I was the youngest inspector in the history of the Italian police force. The first case I solved . . . Do you remember Matera? Or were you too young?"

"I read about it later in the newspapers. Filippo Matera, the 'Monster of Orvieto.'"

"Indeed. Good for you . . . I nabbed him. It was a sensational case. At least the few facts the newspapers reported made it seem that way . . . Mussolini himself sent me his regards. Then came September 8th, the Chief of Police went into hiding and I was left to run the show, me and another officer and that's all. After two days the Germans arrived and Rassetto with them. So, I ended up in an office that worked, that was efficient, doing my job as a police officer as it should be done, just like before. There's a case to be solved, somebody to be found? I solve it, and I find them. Never tortured a soul, never seen anybody tortured . . . You don't believe me? Well, go ahead and think what you want. I wasn't in the Political Squad because I was a fascist, I was there for the same reason that a lot of other people were. I didn't give a good goddamn about—"

"Right, you were only doing your job—"

"No, not my job, Leonardi, my profession! It's different—"

"Yeah, it's different. It's even worse."

De Luca's face twisted and he threw his arms open, leaning back in the chair.

"Fine. Let's put judgments aside for now; it's not the right moment. Those grenades of yours aren't going to keep us alive for much longer, so let's just make sure we get ourselves out of this mess, shall we?"

He stood and began pacing the room, hands in his pockets. Leonardi saw his chance and took his chair back.

"There are a lot of dark corners in this case," said De Luca, "starting with this Baroncini character, who's got nothing to do with anything but is all over the place and is always running off like he has something to hide. Did you get that information I asked you for?"

"Yeah. He paid for the two trucks in Italian lire, in cash, up front. The same day he also bought a piece of land, which, however, isn't worth a thing because it's full of land mines."

"It must be worth something. Baroncini doesn't seem like the kind of man who throws money away. Baroncini went to the count's house the night he was killed, but not with Carnera. Baroncini knows something important and he's afraid; he's always on the run and he gets Bedeschi to tell me to leave him alone. Why? Always been a mystery, and a mystery it remains. Now to Carnera . . . let me sit down, if you don't mind."

Leonardi stood up instinctively and De Luca sat down.

Leonardi opened his mouth to say something but De Luca started talking again.

"So, Carnera and his GAP go to the count's villa to liquidate . . . to execute the count. All according to plan, except for the fact that Carnera is prey to a moment of weakness and he drops the brooch and the ring into his pocket. Then, out of the blue, something goes wrong. Everyone out of there quick! What was in that house that was so terrible? Ghosts? And it had to be something hefty because the Topolino wasn't big enough, they needed Gianni's van . . . and above all," De Luca rapped his knuckles against the wooden table, "something dangerous, so much so they had to keep Delmo quiet with the brooch, though not for long. What could possibly scare a man like Carnera?"

Leonardi didn't say a word and De Luca nodded.

"Right. Nothing scares Carnera. He's a hero, and that's not all: a hero who thinks deeply about power relationships. If not, he would have killed me that day in the yard. And Carnera knows perfectly well that here, he's the one with the most power." De Luca rapped his knuckles on the table again and fell back in the chair, folding his arms across his chest. Leonardi waited until he could no longer resist.

"And so?"

"So, we need to find the count. Whatever it was that scared Carnera is buried with him."

Leonardi bit his lip, put his hands on his hips, turned his head to the side, and looked out the window.

"I'm waiting, Brigadier," said De Luca.

"Look, Engineer, I don't know where the count is buried. There are people in a lot of places around here: along the river banks, behind the count's villa—"

"No, not behind the villa. They needed a van for the move . . . We need a place where not many people go, a place that's not very well known, not very accessible and reasonably far away. Do you know of any places like that, Brigadier?"

Leonardi was still looking out the window. He shook his head and then opened his mouth.

"Oh yes, yes there is a place like that! Carnera buried a German there once! Good lord, Engineer . . . It's the field that Baroncini bought!"

CHAPTER THIRTEEN

"Are you sure that map is right?"

"Relax, Engineer, it was given to us by a deserter and it's never failed. Just make sure you stay right behind me."

De Luca moved awkwardly, one foot behind the other, holding his spade like a tightrope walker. His shoes sank into the soft earth, still wet from the rainfall a few days earlier.

"We're in luck," said Leonardi. "The land mines mean there's less terrain to search . . . There are no more after that ditch."

They jumped across the ditch and stood on the other side. Leonardi sighed with relief, dropping his spade and a stake and leaning his arms across the machine gun that was slung over his shoulder. There was a small artillery emplacement in the middle of the field with grass growing up through the cracks in the concrete.

"It was an artillery post with an 88-millimeter anti-aircraft gun," said Leonardi. "They cut down that tree because it interfered with the line of fire. So? Where do we start? It'll be dark soon, Engineer."

De Luca stepped up onto the concrete emplacement, his fists on his hips, and looked around. Although the land mines cut down on the terrain, the area that remained was still a lot for two people.

"Have a look over there," said Leonardi, pointing to a heap of freshly dug earth just beyond the edge of the concrete. "Somebody's already tried to dig there."

De Luca nodded. "Baroncini," he said. "But I don't think the count is buried close to the concrete . . . Water runs off the emplacement right there whenever it rains and Carnera is no fool. Let's exclude the edges." He squinted because Leonardi was right; the light was fading, quickly. "When somebody hides something, even forever, they tend to work from a reference point . . . That cut tree. Let's start there."

He stepped down and picked up the stake, a wooden stick, long and thin like a javelin. He walked over to the tree trunk and stopped to think.

"How far do you think the roots extend?" he asked.

"At least up to here." Leonardi made a line on the ground with his boot and De Luca planted the stake, pushing it down deep with two hands. Leonardi watched him, serious, worried.

"I don't like being around dead people when they're buried," he said. "They give me the creeps."

"The living scare me more," said De Luca. He pulled the stake out, leaving a round hole in the ground and then made another one next to the first and another and yet another, circling the tree trunk. He had almost got to the end when he stopped. The stake quivered, planted halfway.

"There's something here."

"Oh God!"

De Luca picked up the spade and began digging near the stake, digging quickly, frantic, stopping only to take off his trench coat and throw it down at the base of the trunk.

"So?" he said to Leonardi. "Are you going to help me?"

Leonardi grimaced and slipped the machine gun off his shoulder. He picked up his spade and started to dig too, but slower, moving the earth delicately, and far from the stake. It was getting dark.

"Get the flashlight and give me some light," said De Luca, stopping to dry the sweat dripping from his brow. Now he took off his jacket and rolled up his shirtsleeves, rubbing his hands, which were starting to hurt.

"They might have buried him three meters deep," said Leonardi. "There were two of them and maybe they dug all night . . . Maybe what you hit was a rock, or a piece of—"

"There! Look there!"

De Luca stopped and planted the spade in the ground at the edge of the hole. He knelt down and started digging with his hands. He scraped the dirt away from a length of dark fabric.

"Brigadier, light please!"

He tried pulling, with all his strength, and the fabric came free from the earth, sending him off balance. It was a bundle of fabric, rolled up and bound with a plaited cord.

"What is it? What is it?"

De Luca stepped out of the hole and sat down on the tree trunk. He loosened the cord and opened the fabric over the trunk, brushing away the soil.

"A dressing gown," he said. "The count's dressing gown. We're on to something, Brigadier. We're on to something!"

A strange crumpling sound, different from the rustling of the dusty fabric, stopped his hand as it was moving over one of the dressing gown's pockets. He reached beneath the satin edge with two fingers and pulled out a piece of paper.

"What is it?" Leonardi repeated. "What is it?"

De Luca took him by the hand and guided the beam of light onto the paper. It was a receipt; two hundred thousand lire made out to the Sant'Alberto CLN in the name of Count Amedeo Pasini.

"Two hundred thousand?" said Leonardi. "The CLN never received two hundred thousand lire . . . Some fascists went and supported the CLN at the end, to save their skin, but beside the fact that they were killed anyway I never heard anything about this donation."

"Look who signed the receipt."

"Oh Christ! Baroncini!"

"There's how he found the money for the trucks . . . And that's why he was involved with the count and why he bought this land. He wanted to get the receipt back, and the count always kept it in his pocket, understandably. If Carnera had known about this it'd be Baroncini lying under the earth at this point. That's why he took off."

De Luca folded the piece of paper and gave it to Leonardi. Then he stood up and went back to the hole. He began digging again where the dressing gown had left its imprint, stopping to scrape away dirt with the edge of the spade whenever he thought he felt something. It was Leonardi, who, with a stifled groan, sending the torchlight bouncing around madly, first noticed a livid knee, bluish under the light of the moon.

"Oh, dear God!"

De Luca dropped the spade and started digging with his hands, like a dog, turning his head over his shoulder in Leonardi's direction.

"Well, Brigadier? Do you want to be a police officer or not?"

Leonardi stepped down into the hole but he didn't touch anything. He stood there holding the flashlight until De Luca straightened up, wiping his hands on his trousers.

"Who is this? Is it the count?"

Leonardi looked at the half-buried face sticking up out of the disturbed earth.

"Yes," he said, covering his mouth as he retched. "Yes, it's him."

"Good. As you can see, he is naked. And as you may note, unless the count had three legs, there is another body underneath. And from what they say about the count, and the fact that this second body is also naked, I would guess they were in bed together. That's why Carnera needed a van: he killed two of them in the villa that night. Brigadier, if you must vomit, please do it outside this hole. It's disgusting enough in here already."

Leonardi handed De Luca the flashlight and climbed out in a hurry. He bent over the tree trunk and opened his mouth, holding his stomach with one hand. De Luca trained the beam of light down into the hole and the two bodies, twisted together, white, gleaming under the dark earth, like marble.

"All right," he said to himself. "All right. But there's still something missing. What was so terrible that it could scare Carnera?"

Something caught his eye, reflecting the light for a second, something lying in the dirt beside a lock of blond hair. There was something there, buried beneath a clump of earth, something that De Luca dug up with his fingers and nails, in the dark, because he had dropped the flashlight.

"Oh God," he murmured when he had it in his hand. "Oh God!" he repeated when he turned the torchlight on it. "Sissi!"

Leonardi lifted his head up, spitting out the final threads of saliva.

"Sissi? The dog?" he said, hoarse.

"Oh no, no . . ." A tense, hysterical smile had deformed his face and De Luca could hardly speak. "No, Brigadier, no . . ." He lifted up a creased coat belonging to a military uniform and turned the flashlight onto the white name strip right next to the shoulder flashes.

"Sissi is no dog. He's a Polish officer!"

CHAPTER FOURTEEN

"Carnera shot himself, Engineer. The minute we got to his house with the carabinieri and the Poles, he put a pistol under his chin and pulled the trigger."

De Luca was sitting on a stool, his back against the wall of the cell and a newspaper on his knees. A woman had been there early that morning and had cleaned the floor and sprayed disinfectant on the walls, which now smelled of pure alcohol. Leonardi winced, disgusted, and threw the door open. He sat on the cot next to De Luca.

"The Poles arrived and took their Sissi away with them," he said. "And that's that. I wrote a report, three copies, one for me, one for the Polish military police and one for the carabinieri." He pulled a form out of his pocket, folded in four. "I wrote down everything: Carnera who goes to the count's, Carnera who kills the fellow and only then realizes that he's a Polish officer, Delmo Guerra who sees him burying the bodies in Bedeschi's bottom fields and who blackmails him threatening him with the only thing that could scare him, the involvement of the Allies, and Carnera who first pays him and then wipes out the entire family. The MP captain took the report and then did this." Leonardi tore the report in two, lengthways, and then joined the two halves. "So, the carabinieri maresciallo said 'yes, sir' and did this." He tore the report in the other direction and threw the pieces into the air. One shred came tumbling down through the air and landed on his shoulder.

"Understandable," said De Luca. "It's an embarrassing turn of events."

"Right. This way everyone's happy. Savioli and Bedeschi have got Carnera out of their hair. Baroncini, too! He's back from Bologna and he donated new windowpanes to the school."

"And you, Brigadier? Are you happy?"

"I don't know. I don't know if I'm happy. The carabinieri said the police needed people like me, but they didn't mean that I was good at my job. They meant that I was dependable." Leonardi shook his head, pursing his lips. Then he shrugged.

"But, yes, I'm happy. This is what I wanted. But I'm sorry about Carnera."

De Luca looked at his hands, fingering the blisters on his palms, swollen and smooth. He wasn't used to digging.

"This is not a moral battle between the good guys and the bad guys, Brigadier," he said. "For us, homicide is simply a physical fact, a question of legal responsibility. Your Carnera made a mistake and mistakes must be paid for." He realized that Leonardi was looking at him with a strange expression on his face, making him feel uncomfortable.

"I'm glad you think that way, Engineer," he said, lowering his gaze. "Because the Poles have gone . . . but the carabinieri are still here."

De Luca opened his mouth as the newspaper fell from his knees.

"By now everybody knows who you are," said Leonardi. "I couldn't hide it any longer. And, good God, Engineer . . ."

De Luca looked around, disorientated, and bit his lip. He let out a short sigh that was almost a whine. Fear had contracted his stomach. He lowered his eyes and swallowed.

"Well, yes . . ." he murmured. "Yes, maybe it's better . . . This way I can clear things up . . . I can clear everything up . . ."

"Right. Of course . . ." said Leonardi. "That's the trick . . . A good lawyer, a good defense . . . You'll see, Engineer, everything will work out."

They looked each other in the eye, each nodding, avoiding looking at the newspaper that had fallen onto the floor, and its front page headline: "Special Supreme Court Commission: Murderer Rassetto Sentenced to Death."

"Engineer . . ." said Leonardi. "Commissario . . ." But just then footsteps in the corridor made both men jump to their feet. A carabiniere wearing a light-colored uniform from a country post looked in the door. Another waited behind him. The first man brusquely handed Leonardi a document.

"Let's hurry it up, Brigadier," he said. "I don't care at all for the way those people out there have been looking at us . . . Outside, a madwoman with short hair spat on us and was about to throw stones at us. Sign this paper, if you would. And him?"

He pointed at De Luca who was standing against the wall and the other carabiniere took a step forward, his hands in his pockets. He grabbed De Luca by his coat sleeve and quickly closed a pair of handcuffs around his wrists. De Luca looked up at Leonardi, a pale smile trembling on his lips.

"It's . . . It's my first time," he murmured.

"C'mon, let's go," said the carabiniere. They took him by the arms and pushed him out, almost holding him off the ground.

"Go easy," said Leonardi, extending his arm. But by then they were already out. He was alone in the cell, the release papers in his hand, lost, until he roused himself and ran to his office.

He got to the window in time to see them shoving De Luca into the wagon with its canvas flaps drawn, looking this way and that, quick and wary, machine guns in their hands.

Carlo Lucarelli is one of Italy's best-loved crime writers. He was born in Parma in 1960. His publishing debut came with the extremely successful "De Luca Trilogy" in 1990 and he has since published over a dozen novels and collections of stories. He is an active member of several Italian and international writer's associations, and he teaches at Alessandro Baricco's Holden School in Turin and in Padua's maximum-security prison. Several of his novels have been translated into French for Gallimard's renowned "Noir" series. He conducts the program "Blue Night" on Italian network television, and his novels *Almost Blue* and *Lupo Mannaro* have both been made into films.

About Europa Editions

"To insist that if work is good, no matter what, people will read it? Crazy! But perhaps that's why I like Europa . . . They believe in what they are doing above everything. Viva Europa Editions!"
—ALICE SEBOLD, author of *The Lovely Bones*

"A new and, on first evidence, excellent source for European fiction for English-speaking readers."—JANET MASLIN, *The New York Times*

"Europa Editions has its first indie bestseller, Elena Ferrante's *The Days of Abandonment*."—*Publishers Weekly*

"We certainly like what we've seen so far."—*The Complete Review*

"A distinctly different brand of literary pleasure, thoughtfulness and, yes, even entertainment."—*The Ruminator*

"You could consider Europa Editions, the sprightly new publishing venture [...] based in New York, as a kind of book club for Americans who thirst after exciting foreign fiction."—*LA Weekly*

"Europa Editions invites English-speaking readers to 'experience all the color, the exuberance, the violence, the sounds and smells of the Mediterranean,' with an intriguing selection of the crème de la crème of continental noir."—*Murder by the Bye*

"Readers with a taste—even a need—for an occasional inky cup of bitter honesty should lap up *The Goodbye Kiss* . . . the first book of Carlotto's to be published in the United States by the increasingly impressive new Europa Editions."—*Chicago Tribune*

www.europaeditions.com

The Days of Abandonment
Elena Ferrante
Fiction - 192 pp - $14.95 - isbn 978-1-933372-00-6

"Stunning . . . The raging, torrential voice of the author is something rare."—*The New York Times*

"I could not put this novel down. Elena Ferrante will blow you away."
—ALICE SEBOLD, author of *The Lovely Bones*

The gripping story of a woman's descent into devastating emptiness after being abandoned by her husband with two young children to care for.

Troubling Love
Elena Ferrante
Fiction - 144 pp - $14.95 - isbn 978-1-933372-16-7

"In tactile, beautifully restrained prose, Ferrante makes the domestic violence that tore [the protagonist's] household apart evident."—*Publishers Weekly*

"Ferrante has written the 'Great Neapolitan Novel.'"
—*Corriere della Sera*

Delia's voyage of discovery through the chaotic streets and claustrophobic sitting rooms of contemporary Naples in search of the truth about her mother's untimely death.

Cooking with Fernet Branca
James Hamilton-Paterson
Fiction - 288 pp - $14.95 - isbn 978-1-933372-01-3

"Provokes the sort of indecorous involuntary laughter that has more in common with sneezing than chuckling. Imagine a British John Waters crossed with David Sedaris."—*The New York Times*

Gerald Samper has his own private Tuscan hilltop where he whiles away his time working as a ghostwriter for celebrities and inventing wholly original culinary concoctions. His idyll is shattered by the arrival of Marta. A series of hilarious misunderstandings brings this odd couple into ever-closer proximity.

Old Filth
Jane Gardam
Fiction - 256 pp - $14.95 - isbn 978-1-933372-13-6

"This remarkable novel [...] will bring immense pleasure to readers who treasure fiction that is intelligent, witty, sophisticated and—a quality encountered all too rarely in contemporary culture—adult."—*The Washington Post*

The engrossing and moving account of the life of Sir Edward Feathers, from birth in colonial Malaya, to Wales, where he is sent as a "Raj orphan," to Oxford, his career and marriage, parallels much of the twentieth century's dramatic history.

Total Chaos
Jean-Claude Izzo
Fiction/Noir - 256 pp - $14.95 - isbn 978-1-933372-04-4

"Rich, ambitious and passionate . . . his sad, loving portrait of his native city is amazing."—*The Washington Post*

"Full of fascinating characters, tersely brought to life in a prose style that is (thanks to Howard Curtis's shrewd translation) traditionally dark and completely original."—*The Chicago Tribune*

The first installment in the Marseilles Trilogy.

Chourmo
Jean-Claude Izzo
Fiction/Noir - 256 pp - $14.95 - isbn 978-1-933372-17-4

"Like the best noir writers—and he is among the best—Izzo not only has a keen eye for detail but also digs deep into what makes men weep."—*Time Out New York*

Montale is dragged back into the mean streets of a violent, crime-infested Marseilles after the disappearance of his long lost cousin's teenage son.

The Goodbye Kiss
Massimo Carlotto
Fiction/Noir - 192 pp - $14.95 - isbn 978-1-933372-05-1

"A nasty, explosive little tome warmly recommended to fans of James M. Cain for its casual amorality and truly astonishing speed."—*Kirkus Reviews*

An unscrupulous womanizer, as devoid of morals now as he once was full of idealistic fervor, returns to Italy, where he is wanted for a series of crimes. To avoid prison he sells out his old friends, turns his back on his former ideals, and cuts deals with crooked cops. To earn himself the guise of respectability he is willing to go even further, maybe even as far as murder.

Death's Dark Abyss
Massimo Carlotto
Fiction/Noir - 192 pp - $14.95 - isbn 978-1-933372-18-1

"A narrative voice that in Lawrence Venuti's translation is cold and heartless—but, in a creepy way, fascinating."—*The New York Times*

A riveting drama of guilt, revenge, and justice, Massimo Carlotto's *Death's Dark Abyss* tells the story of two men and the savage crime that binds them. During a robbery, Raffaello Beggiato takes a young woman and her child hostage and later murders them. Beggiato is arrested, tried, and sentenced to life. The victims' father and husband, Silvano, plunges into a deepening abyss until the day the murderer seeks his pardon and he begins to plot his revenge.

Hangover Square
Patrick Hamilton
Fiction/Noir - 280 pp - $14.95 - isbn 978-1-933372-06-8

"Hamilton is a sort of urban Thomas Hardy: always a pleasure to read, and as social historian he is unparalleled."—NICK HORNBY

Adrift in the grimy pubs of London at the outbreak of World War II, George Harvey Bone is hopelessly infatuated with Netta, a cold, contemptuous small-time actress. George also suffers from occasional blackouts. During these moments one thing is horribly clear: he must murder Netta.

Boot Tracks
Matthew F. Jones
Fiction/Noir - 208 pp - $14.95 - isbn 978-1-933372-11-2

"More than just a very good crime thriller, this dark but illuminating novel shows us the psychopathology of the criminal mind . . . A nightmare thriller with the power to haunt."
—*Kirkus Reviews* (starred)

A commanding, stylishly written novel that tells the harrowing story of an assassination gone terribly wrong and the man and woman who are taking their last chance to find a safe place in a hostile world.

Love Burns
Edna Mazya
Fiction/Noir - 192 pp - $14.95 - isbn 978-1-933372-08-2

"This book, which has Woody Allen overtones, should be of great interest to readers of black humor and psychological thrillers."
—*Library Journal* (starred)

Ilan, a middle-aged professor of astrophysics, discovers that his young wife is having an affair. Terrified of losing her, he decides to confront her lover instead. Their meeting ends in the latter's murder—the unlikely murder weapon being Ilan's pipe—and in desperation, Ilan disposes of the body in the fresh grave of his kindergarten teacher. But when the body is discovered, the mayhem begins.

Departure Lounge
Chad Taylor
Fiction/Noir - 176 pp - $14.95 - isbn 978-1-933372-09-9

"Smart, original, surprising and just about as cool as a novel can get . . . Taylor can flat out write."—*The Washington Post*

A young woman mysteriously disappears. The lives of those she has left behind—family, acquaintances, and strangers intrigued by her disappearance—intersect to form a captivating latticework of coincidences and surprising twists of fate. Urban noir at its stylish and intelligent best.

The Big Question
Wolf Erlbruch
Children's Illustrated Fiction - 52 pp - $14.95 - isbn 978-1-933372-03-7

Named Best Book at the 2004 Children's Book Fair in Bologna.

"[*The Big Question*] offers more open-ended answers than the likes
of Shel Silverstein's *Giving Tree* (1964) and is certain to leave even
younger readers in a reflective mood."—*Kirkus Reviews*

A stunningly beautiful and poetic illustrated book for children that
poses the biggest of all big questions: Why am I here?

The Butterfly Workshop
Wolf Erlbruch
Children's Illustrated Fiction - 40 pp - $14.95 - isbn 978-1-933372-12-9

Illustrated by the winner of the 2006 Hans Christian Andersen
Award.

For children and adults alike: Odair, one of the Designers of All
Things and grandson of the esteemed inventor of the rainbow, has
been banished to the insect laboratory as punishment for his over-
active imagination. But he still dreams of one day creating a cross
between a bird and a flower.

Carte Blanche
Carlo Lucarelli
Fiction/Noir - 128 pp - $14.95 - isbn 978-1-933372-15-0

"This is Alan Furst country, to be sure."—*Booklist*

The house of cards built by Mussolini in the last months of World War II is collapsing and Commissario De Luca faces a world mired in sadistic sex, dirty money, drugs and murder.

Dog Day
Alicia Giménez-Bartlett
Fiction/Noir - 208 pp - $14.95 - isbn 978-1-933372-14-3

"In Nicholas Caistor's smooth translation from the Spanish, Giménez-Bartlett evokes pity, horror and laughter with equal adeptness. No wonder she won the Femenino Lumen prize in 1997 as the best female writer in Spain."—*The Washington Post*

Delicado and her maladroit sidekick, Garzón, investigate the murder of a tramp whose only friend is a mongrel dog named Freaky.